Mark of Fate

The Chronicles of Kerrigan, Volume 9

W.J. May

Published by Dark Shadow Publishing, 2016.

MARK OF FATE

First edition. March 26, 2016.

Written by W.J. May.

Also by W.J. May

Bit-Lit Series
Lost Vampire
Cost of Blood
Price of Death

Blood Red Series
Courage Runs Red
The Night Watch
Marked by Courage

Daughters of Darkness: Victoria's Journey
Huntress
Coveted (A Vampire & Paranormal Romance)
Victoria

Hidden Secrets Saga
Seventh Mark - Part 1
Seventh Mark - Part 2
Marked By Destiny
Compelled
Fate's Intervention
Chosen Three

The Chronicles of Kerrigan
Rae of Hope
Dark Nebula
House of Cards
Royal Tea
Under Fire
End in Sight

Hidden Darkness
Twisted Together
Mark of Fate

The Chronicles of Kerrigan Prequel
Christmas Before the Magic

The Hidden Secrets Saga
Seventh Mark (part 1 & 2)

The Senseless Series
Radium Halos
Radium Halos - Part 2
Nonsense

The X Files
Code X
Replica X

Standalone
Shadow of Doubt (Part 1 & 2)
Five Shades of Fantasy
Glow - A Young Adult Fantasy Sampler
Shadow of Doubt - Part 2
Four and a Half Shades of Fantasy
Full Moon
Dream Fighter
What Creeps in the Night
Forest of the Forbidden
HuNted
Arcane Forest: A Fantasy Anthology
Ancient Blood of the Vampire and Werewolf

The Chronicles of Kerrigan

Mark of Fate

Book IX

By

W.J. May

The Chronicles of Kerrigan

Book I - *Rae of Hope* **is FREE!**
Book Trailer:
http://www.youtube.com/watch?v=gILAwXxx8MU
Book II - *Dark Nebula*
Book Trailer:
http://www.youtube.com/watch?v=Ca24STi_bFM
Book III - *House of Cards*
Book IV - *Royal Tea*
Book V - *Under Fire*
Book VI - *End in Sight*
Book VII – *Hidden Darkness*
Book VIII – *Twisted Together*
Book IX – *Mark of Fate*
Book X – *Strength & Power*
Coming April 2016
Book XI – *Last One Standing*
Coming May 2016
Book XII – *Rae of Light*
Coming June 2016
PREQUEL – Christmas Before the Magic

Chronicles of Kerrigan Prequel

A Novella of the Chronicles of Kerrigan.
A prequel on how Simon Kerrigan met Beth!!
AVAILABLE:

Find W.J. May

Website:
http://www.wanitamay.yolasite.com

Facebook:
https://www.facebook.com/pages/Author-WJ-May-FAN-PAGE/141170442608149

Newsletter:
SIGN UP FOR W.J. May's Newsletter to find out about new releases, updates, cover reveals and even freebies!

http://eepurl.com/97aYf

W.J. May

Description:

Mark of Fate is the 9th Book of W.J. May's bestselling series, The Chronicles of Kerrigan.

"Life doesn't always make sense, and the heart doesn't always understand what the head realizes."

Rae Kerrigan has proven herself a vital asset to the Privy Council and yet, they still question her loyalty.

Back in London, Rae returns to find that everything isn't exactly as it seems. The Privy Council may be officially offering her and her friends their jobs back, but not everyone is as eager to call a truce.

Sides are chosen. Lines are drawn in the sand. Rae finds herself torn, not only between two futures, but between two loves.

When an object left behind from her father exposes a ghastly secret, Rae find herself faced with the toughest question of all.

Can there ever be a happy ending for a Kerrigan?

Mark of Fate is the 9th book in the Chronicles of Kerrigan series.

Book 1, Rae of Hope is currently FREE.

Follow Rae Kerrigan as she learns about the tattoo on her back that gives her supernatural powers, as she learns of her father's evil intentions and as she tries to figure out how coming of age, falling love and high-packed action fighting isn't as easy as the comic books make it look.

<u>Series Order:</u>

Rae of Hope

Dark Nebula

House of Cards

Royal Tea

Chapter 1

'When everything goes to hell, the people who stand by you without flinching—they are your family.'
— Jim Butcher

Unless you're a Kerrigan. In that case, the ones raising hell are most likely your family...

"What are you doing in my mother's house?" Rae said the words slowly, carefully, stepping strategically around the table as she spoke as to put her body in between her mother and Kraigan. Yes, she was the one who had initiated contact this time, but she had also initiated contact last time and she'd thought they all remembered with painful clarity how well that had gone.

Kraigan answered her question with a wicked, perfect smile. "Aww, come on, Rae. Is that any way to greet your little brother?" He opened his arms wide. "Give us a hug."

No one moved.

"Why?" Molly hissed from by the door. "So you can steal a tatù from her?" Her fingers crackled with an electric warning as she folded her arms menacingly across her chest. On either side of her, Devon and Julian both took a threatening step forward.

Oh yes...they all remembered how well it had gone last time.

"That's adorable," Kraigan looked the petite redhead up and down. "Kitty has claws."

"What are you doing in *my* mother's house?" Rae asked again, more deliberately this time.

"*Kitty has—*" Molly threw down her purse and lifted her hands into the air. "Oh, that's it!"

Kraigan burst out laughing, dropping back into a casual fighting stance.

Except, before either one could move a muscle, Julian stepped between them, his eyes flashing dangerously.

"You don't win."

Don't. Not *won't*.

Julian had a special way of knowing these things for sure, and because it was Julian saying it, Kraigan actually took a step back, straightening up as if he'd never meant to fight in the first place.

Devon folded his arms across his chest with a smug smile. "Not so cocky now that you don't have a gun on you, eh? Rae's little brother?"

A shattering sound erupted by the fireplace as an empty coffee mug slipped from Beth's hands. "You pulled a *gun* on—"

"KRAIGAN!"

All the sound in the room stopped cold as everyone turned in unison to look at Rae.

She stood with her hands resting lightly on her hips, a single eyebrow raised in accusation. "*My* mother's house?"

Kraigan's lips turned up in a sarcastic smile. "Well, we couldn't very well meet at *my* mother's house, could we?"

You could have heard a drop after that.

He glanced blandly around the room at the five identical looks of shock. "What? Too soon?"

Rae closed her eyes for a split second, then took a seat at the table, deliberately trying to slow the pace of the conversation before things could get too heated. She'd almost forgotten what a certifiable psychopath her half-brother was. *A bit like Gabriel.*

She kicked that thought out of her head and once she was settled, she kicked out the chair across from her and gestured for Kraigan to sit. "Well, I see someone's already bouncing back from the truth about their mother's untimely death..."

"Not really." He eyed the chair carefully for a moment, before settling himself down in one graceful movement. He may try to act unconcerned, flippant even—but Kraigan wasn't stupid. Even he had to realize the firepower he was up against by stepping into this house. He was Simon Kerrigan's son, after all. "Actually, that's kind of what I came to talk to you about."

"Oh, and here I thought you came for a summer picnic," Molly grumbled.

Rae held up a hand to cut her off, leaning across the table with sudden interest. "You found her?"

Kraigan nodded slowly, keeping his eyes locked on Rae all the while. "I did."

Rae guessed she shouldn't be so surprised. Jennifer Jones may have been one of the greatest inked super-agents on the planet, but Kraigan was his own brand of crazy. And when channeled into something as powerful as revenge, Rae couldn't see too many things getting in the way of him and his target. It was the reason she had come to him in the first place. "Of course you did," she breathed.

His mouth turned up in the faintest of smiles, and a second later Rae realized she was smiling herself; grinning even, a feeling of dark anticipation fluttering away in her stomach. "Damn, Kraigan." Her brows pressed together. "Is she dead?"

"Not yet."

Devon glanced between the two with an almost worried expression. "Much as I hate to break up this first-ever moment of sibling bonding..." He yanked out the chair in between them and let it drop to the floor with a loud clatter. The sound of it snapped both brother and sister out of their shared vengeful trance. "You want to tell us why you bailed out and let the trail go cold? You know, a while ago they invented these little things called cell phones."

Rae's forehead creased with a sudden frown. Devon was right. Why on earth would Kraigan have taken his eyes off Jennifer for even a second?

"Devon," Kraigan sighed, running his hands up through his curly brown hair, "still exactly the same as the first time I met you at Guilder. Running around after this one," he jerked his head in Rae's direction, "just trying to keep pace."

Devon opened his mouth for a sharp retort, but Kraigan beat him to it.

"To answer your question, I didn't let the trail go cold. I followed it," he paused for dramatic effect, "right here."

The second he said the words, several things happened at once.

Julian collapsed suddenly into the nearest chair, his eyes glassing over to the iridescent white they took on when he was scanning the future. Molly and Beth immediately crouched down under the line of the windows. And like they'd synchronized it, Devon and Rae flipped over the kitchen table to provide a barricade between the people inside and the door.

It was a blur of speed—lasting only about three seconds.

Kraigan was still blinking around in surprise. His mouth opened and he had to close it as he glanced around the suddenly defensible kitchen, and for the first time Rae had ever seen he flushed with what looked like a hint of embarrassment.

"...to *Scotland*. Not to this house."

He met their furious looks rather sheepishly before lowering his eyes to the floor.

"Oops. Maybe I should've led with that."

Rae banged her forehead against the table as the rest of them slowly relaxed their strategic positions. "*Kraigan.*" She would have slapped the backside of his head if he had been within reach, and been assured he wouldn't absorb one of her tatùs.

"I know. I said oops."

Devon glared as he got to his feet. "Over-theatrical son of a—"

"Get over it," Kraigan snapped.

That was the only apology they were going to get. *Oops*. Rae sensed that the one-time-only 'apologizing' portion of his life was over.

"So, I followed her here to Scotland. At first I wasn't sure why she'd bother," he glanced outside at the stunning moonlit vista with disdain, "I mean, what a dump, right? But then I remembered from a file that I'd stolen from the Privy Council—"

"You *stole* a Privy Council—" Devon grimaced painfully.

"—that you lived here." Kraigan nodded his head at Beth in what he clearly took to be a gracious manner. "So I thought, why not kill two birds with one stone?"

For the second time in less than a minute, the entire kitchen stopped cold, and then in a whirl- wind, the group of four stood protectively around Beth, all looking at Kraigan like he might explode at any moment.

His eyes flicked around at their faces with a hint of confusion, before he threw back his head with an exasperated sigh. "I didn't mean actually *kill*...it's a freaking expression!"

"The kind that you should avoid entirely whilst in my *mother's* house," Rae hissed icily.

"Oh relax," he yawned, "I don't want to kill your mother. Although that does have a certain symmetry to it..." He tilted back in his chair with a grin as Rae leapt angrily closer to him. *"Relax,"* he said again. "I only meant that not only could I kill the infamous Jennifer Jones, but I could meet the equally infamous Beth Kerrigan. It's an honor." He cocked his head and studied her curiously. "Talk about case files. Yours kept me reading for half the night. Did you really smuggle a box full of percussion grenades through Colombian customs? I'd love to know how you did that—"

"Enough, Kraigan!" Rae cut him off, feeling suddenly exhausted by all the banter. She'd just stepped off a plane for what felt like the millionth time that summer, having marched into the headquarters of the most powerful tatù alliance in the world, to tell them that not only had she and her friends been running all over the world chasing a mysterious 'not-really-dead' man bent on world domination, but that she was quitting her job once and for all. Oh yeah, and she'd also taken down about half of their greatest guards in the process.

She'd come back to Scotland with the sole purpose of getting yelled at by her mother, and then getting a million nights' worth of sleep. Her plans didn't extend much beyond that point. They certainly didn't include this unexpected run-in with her crazy brother.

Kraigan jutted up his chin, looking affronted. "What the hell happened to you, Rae? I thought you'd be happy to know that I'd tracked down our little traitor like you wanted. Even happier to know that I found out she was coming here—so close to your own mother—so that we could beat her to the punch."

Rae rubbed her temples. "And I am; it's just..."

Her pause had Kraigan speaking instantly again. "In fact, I thought it was damn gentlemanly of me to think to include you in her murder. I could have done it by myself, you know? But I felt like it should be a family affair."

A family affair?

Beth sucked in a sharp breath. She'd stiffened at the mention of Jennifer's name, but hadn't said anything. Rae wondered, but with Kraigan in the room it was hard to take a moment to focus on the why. The rest of the room stared at Kraigan like he was deeply disturbed, but at this point Rae felt as though nothing would shock her. At least he wasn't trying to kill her.

"While I'm grateful you found her," she said more forcibly, "it's just been a long day, and I could do without your colorful Charles Manson kind of commentary, alright?"

"Oh, sis." He scooted his chair beside the one she'd been sitting on and straightened it upright, and then patted the seat. With a coaxing smile, he said, "You're stressed, I can see that. What happened? Tell me all about it." He propped up his chin on his fists and gazed at her with mischievous faux concern; even crossing his legs in an exaggerated fashion.

Valiantly resisting the urge to punch him in the face, Rae sat down and moved her chair back several feet to re-establish the distance between them. The last thing she wanted was Kraigan touching her skin and stealing one of her best tatùs, not with a fight with Jennifer Jones looming on the horizon. "Well, if you must know," she shot him a sarcastic glare, "I just quit my job."

Much to her surprise Kraigan dropped the act at once, straightening up and looking at her with something close to respect. "Really? The Privy Council's prized weapon? Gone rogue?" He grinned. "Maybe you are a Kerrigan after all."

"I'm not going rogue," Rae fired back, painfully aware of the fact that her mother's eyes were upon her and they had yet to discuss this in person. "I'm...taking a step back. Re-evaluating my options."

"Retribution for being arrested," Molly added helpfully.

"*Molls.*"

Again, Kraigan looked at Rae with genuine interest. "They arrested you? This just keeps getting better. Why?"

"It doesn't matter," Devon interjected quickly, stopping the conversation before it could take a dangerous turn.

Kraigan didn't know anything about Cromfield, and as far as they knew Cromfield didn't know anything about Kraigan. It was in everyone's best interests to keep it that way. There was no telling how Kraigan might feel about the 'work' Cromfield had dedicated his life to, but either way it was best to keep two such volatile people at a great distance and well off each other's radar.

Kraigan glanced at Devon as if he'd just stolen his favorite toy. "Fine. You don't trust me. I get it. And while I think that reaction might be a little harsh—"

"You pointed a gun at my head," Molly spat.

"And tried to kill me," Devon growled.

"And me," Rae concluded, adding for good measure, "several times."

"Well, you say potato, I say—"

Julian gritted his teeth. "Maybe it's best you don't say anything, Kraigan."

"My only point is," he bristled, "for once you were right, big sister. Our interests are, however temporarily, aligned. I'm not going to do anything to hurt you and your little band of outlaws. Not while the woman who killed my mother is still at large."

There was a brief pause.

"And once we've taken care of her?" Rae asked carefully.

He folded his hands behind his head with a casual shrug. "Who knows? We can take it one day at a time."

"That's it," Devon muttered under his breath, "I can't take any more of this." He put his hand on Rae's shoulder. "We know Jennifer's in Scotland. We can find her. We don't need...*him.*"

Kraigan grinned. "Oh, but I'm afraid you do. You see, even with my not inconsiderable resources, it still took me months to find her, and as it turned out, that entire time she was right there in London. If you think you can do what I couldn't and narrow down her location in an entire country, please, be my guest. But I'm guessing it won't end well."

Devon's eyes narrowed. "And you expect us to believe you showed up here just out of the goodness of your blackened heart? You might be able to find her, but you need us to help you take her down. It's not something you can do on your own, and we all know it."

A muscle twitched in Kraigan's jaw, but he gave away nothing. "Believe what you like. Either way, I'm here now and I'm promising to be good... At least until the mission is over and Jones is cold and in the ground."

Rae shuddered to hear him talk about death so easily, even if it was about someone who deserved it. Unlike her brother, she had never hunted down a person to kill them in cold blood. Aside from Cromfield, that is. Even then, when she thought about the act, the actual moment when the two of them would inevitably face off...it disturbed her greatly. As much as she hated to admit it, Kraigan was right. She had asked him to help for a reason. Jennifer was a ticking time bomb, and to take her out they needed each other. There was no way around it.

"So we good?" he asked cheerfully. He met their looks of sour resignation with a grin. "See? One big happy family. And in a show of good faith, I'm even going to tell you that there's what looks like the remains of an Englishman bleeding out on your front porch."

For a second, no one moved. Then everyone looked slowly at the door.

"The remains of..." Rae trailed off in utter confusion.

Kraigan shrugged indifferently. "Probably one of those tragic singing telegrams."

Julian's eyes flashed momentarily white and he came back looking pale. "Oh shit, Gabriel!"

Gabriel?!

Rae was up on her feet and yanking open the door in the same breath. Sure enough there he was, his hand still half-raised to knock... bleeding a little puddle onto the front stoop.

Her arms were around him before she even realized what she was doing, pressing her body against his and squeezing him in a tight embrace. It wasn't until he gasped softly and winced that she pulled back, terrified she'd hurt him even more.

"I'm so sorry," she exclaimed, stepping back even farther to survey the damage. Out of the corner of her eye she could see Devon watching, and the tops of her cheeks flushed pink.

"Don't apologize," Gabriel panted with a grin. One hand was clutching discreetly at the door frame, but other than that he was standing up on his own. "That's a proper welcome. I should stop by here more often." He was freshly showered and wearing clean clothes, his blond hair spilling into his face like it always did, and the intoxicating smell of citrus goodness drifting off of his skin. But no matter how much he fixed himself up, he still looked like he'd been put through the wringer.

There was a mess of cuts and bruises littering his handsome face, and his normally bronze skin was colored a ghostly white. Even his lips were broken, Rae noted, her eyes lingering on them a second too long as they twisted up into a weak grin.

"I got your call..." he smiled bravely, "so here I am."

After their showdown at Guilder, they had left Gabriel with a doctor Julian knew in the city—one who wasn't strictly tied to the Privy Council and wouldn't ask questions. They didn't want to leave him there alone, but in case the PC decided to go after them after all they didn't want to lead them back to Gabriel. Not to mention the fact that Rae had yet to explain to her mother what was going on, and he was in no way up for a trip to Scotland in his present state.

At least Rae hadn't thought he was. She blanched, still struck by the sickly pallor of his face, and then slowly connected what he was saying. "Wait—call? Who called you?"

"I did," Julian, Devon, and Molly all answered at once.

They looked at each other in surprise and Gabriel laughed.

"Yeah, I got three different texts from the lot of you, every one telling me to come and meet you here at your mum's." He nodded politely to Beth, who smiled warmly and rushed forward to help him inside. "I've never been so popular."

"Gracious!" she exclaimed when she got closer and saw his face. "What on earth happened to you? It's usually Devon we have to get cleaned up..."

Kraigan snickered while Devon flushed at the floor.

"It's nothing, Mrs. K," Gabriel dismissed casually, making a visible effort to act a lot better than he obviously felt. "Just a little karmic comeuppance, that's all."

Beth stared at him blankly.

His gaze slowly drifted over to the rest of them. "You...you guys didn't tell her yet?"

"Uh...no," Rae stepped in quickly, her eyes flashing to Kraigan, "we got a little interrupted."

There was an almost comical moment as Kraigan and Gabriel surveyed each other for the first time. Rae could almost feel Devon seething as he glanced between the two of them, but she and Molly shared a secret grin. The two cockiest turncoats they knew, in the same room together.

Whatever happened next would be...interesting, to say the least.

Chapter 2

"Who're you?" Gabriel asked.

At the same time Kraigan stood and stated, "You another of Rae's strays?"

Both guys eyed each other up and down.

Kraigan nodded at Rae. "Fix the poor bugger. He looks like hell."

"I can't," Rae replied simply. "What about you? Why don't you use whatever tatù you've stolen and fix him?"

Gabriel glanced back and forth between the two of them. He started laughed as he turned to Devon, "You have got to be jokin'! Another Kerrigan?"

Beth turned to grab a towel to press against Gabriel's wound. "He's not mine. He's Simon's."

Kraigan's eyes betrayed him for just a split second. Rae saw and she stepped forward. Her mother hadn't meant the words to sounds harsh; she had just been stating a fact. "Kraigan, this is Gabriel. He used to be on the wrong side. Gabriel, this is my half-brother, Kraigan. He's still trying to figure out which side he's on."

Gabriel grinned. "I like him already."

Devon harrumphed and Kraigan's eyes shot back and forth between Devon and Gabriel. "You two don't get along?" Kraigan asked.

"He's the one with the problem." Gabriel nodded toward Devon.

Kraigan held out his hand. "I'm with you there, mate."

As Gabriel reached out to shake Kraigan's hand, Devon slapped it away.

"Hey!" Gabriel said and shook his sore wrist. "What the—"

"Kraigan's father is Simon Kerrigan. Think about it. Simon's tatù, Rae's tatù... and Kraigan."

"I'd have given it back," Kraigan muttered.

"What? You steal people's tatùs?" Gabriel shook his head.

"I borrow them."

"—and don't give them back until you *borrow* someone else's," Molly snapped.

"If Simon's your dad..." Gabriel noticed Beth's tight-lipped mouth. "Oh! I see. Oh, dear." He tutted. "Your tatù's like Rae's, but different? Just like Simon's alone, or..."

"My mother was inked as well." Kraigan glared at Beth, like it was her fault. Then he sighed.

"A hybrid?"

Kraigan clapped his hands. "Give the guy a medal."

Gabriel stepped forward, his face pale both from his injuries and what his mind was processing. "Did your father know you existed?"

"What the hell? Of course he did!"

Gabriel's head tilted to the side. "Simon knew about you?"

Rae suddenly realized where he was going with this. She glanced at Devon and Julian, seeing that they both were realizing it at the same time. Panic filled her. If Gabriel didn't know about Kraigan, neither did Cromfield. If Kraigan didn't know about Cromfield...

"Crom—"

"Gabriel!" Rae cut him off. "You must be exhausted. And famished! Mom, could you make him a sandwich or something? Devon, maybe you could help Gabriel upstairs to your room. Molly, what about some fresh bandages? We can't let this guy bleed out over the floor here." She forced a fake yawn. "Maybe Kraigan could go out and grab some firewood? I think—"

"It's time we all called it a night," Beth interrupted and moved to the fridge. "I'll make some butties and you guys can all go up to your rooms and settle in. I'd like a few moments to talk to my daughter alone, if that isn't too much to ask. I've missed her."

Nobody argued. Beth looked ready to cry because she'd missed her daughter. They all understood the worry and fear she had probably been going through since they'd left.

Beth cleared her throat when nobody moved. "Needless to say, this little meeting had gone a little off the rails even before Gabriel showed up bleeding on the front stoop. Gabriel looks ready to pass out, and Kraigan, I don't know you very well; if my daughter has issues with you, there's a reason. You can head up to the attic and spend the night on a twin cot up there. The rest of you can tactfully make yourselves scarce so Rae can talk with her mom. NOW!"

Each of them stepped forward to help Gabriel up the stairs and into a bed. Except Kraigan, who stood with his hands crossed over his chest, chuckling. When Beth shot him a look, he hurried up the stairs as well.

Rae stayed in the kitchen and watched her friends and brother retire for the night. The time in London had changed Molly, Julian, and Devon. From the second Gabriel had shown up at their door, half beaten to death by Cromfield, all past sins were forgotten and he was accepted as one of their own. It said a lot that each one of them had independently thought to invite him to Scotland. Only Devon still harbored a well-earned resentment, but even that had been graciously—if temporarily—set aside and reduced to sarcastic teasing and provoked defenses. In a war where the stakes were so high, it was simply unfeasible to leave anyone useful out in the cold, much less someone as useful and sincerely reformed as Gabriel.

Thankfully, her mom seemed to understand this too.

"But he didn't let you fall?" she asked again, verifying it for herself. She and Rae had perched on the sofa in front of a dying fire. In the time it had taken Rae to tell her the story the entire house had fallen asleep, leaving them in peaceful silence.

Rae's eyes drifted thoughtfully to the crackling fireplace as she thought back to her recent Guilder break-in. Little did she know it, but at the time Gabriel had been planning to kill her and take the missing piece of the brainwashing device back to Cromfield. He blamed her for his tragic childhood, raised by Cromfield, and hated her accordingly. There had been a moment when he could have done it. A perfect moment when she was dangling over a thirty-foot drop and had just handed him the piece he so wanted. She remembered his minute hesitation as he had glanced between her and the piece. The infinite pause as his life had changed course forever.

He'd decided to save her.

"No," she said quietly, answering her mother's question, "he didn't let me fall."

Of course there were multiple reasons for this. Secret, intimate reasons she had seen when she used Carter's tatù to wade into his sleeping mind and probe his thoughts.

To say he had feelings for her...would be putting it lightly.

They had completely transformed him—changed him at a fundamental level, altered the very fabric of who he was. This was a man who had never known love, who had never known kindness or what it meant to value something above oneself. When he met Rae his eyes had been opened. A wall he never knew existed had crumbled, allowing him to feel all these things for the first time.

The only trouble was, now, he had these feelings for her. And *no one*—not him, not Rae, and certainly not Rae's boyfriend, was supposed to know.

"Then he made his choice," Beth said simply. Rae looked up in surprise, pleased and incredibly grateful for her mother's evolved take on the situation. Beth saw her looking and shook her head with a sigh. "I can't pretend I'm not furious, but look at the facts: Taken as a child, effectively brainwashed, warped and manipulated every day to do Cromfield's bidding? A part of me can't really blame him." Her voice grew suddenly soft as she, too, stared towards the fire. "A part of me can't really blame Jennifer."

Rae's throat seized up and she curled farther back into the couch. Crazy as it sounded, she knew exactly what her mother meant. Jennifer Jones had wronged them as much as a single person could. She'd accidently killed Rae's father, but more importantly she'd taken away Rae's entire childhood. She'd taken away her mother. Taken away her mother's memories of even having a child. Thanks to Jennifer Jones, it was still a complete novelty—to be sitting on a couch with her mother like it was the most natural thing in the world.

And then of course, there was what she did to Kraigan...

Rae's eyes flicked automatically up to the ceiling, almost as if she could see her brother lying on his cot in the attic. Not sleeping, surely. But plotting. Scheming. Fantasizing his revenge.

He may have walked in with his usual sarcastic jokes and swagger, but he couldn't fool her. She was there the day he found out how his mother had really died. She was the one who'd told him. She remembered the look on his face. Pale. Lost. Inconsolable. Like he was four years old again and suddenly found himself an orphan. Left to fend for himself in a dangerous world.

It was unforgivable. Unpardonable. And, most importantly, it was never going to stop.

According to Kraigan, Jennifer had set up shop in a little town on the opposite coast. Far enough away that he begrudgingly accepted Rae's demand that they set out in the morning, but close enough to reveal a simple truth.

Jennifer would never stop hunting them. And for that she had to be destroyed.

"I know, Mom. But it's not as simple as all that..."

She dropped her head on her mother's shoulder and Beth sighed again.

"No..." she stroked back Rae's hair, "it isn't."

Both of them stared into the flickering flames, thinking about the past and the future. About times lost and times to come. Thinking about what the next day would bring. The good and the inevitably bad.

Chapter 3

"Wake up, Rae! Wake up and see what fresh hell is waiting for us."

Rae opened her eyes and shrieked as Molly's murderous face loomed over her. "*What the—!*"

The little fashionista was perched on the edge of the mattress, wearing nothing but a towel, a pair of fluffy shower slippers, and a homicidal scowl.

"Molls? What is it?!" Her first thought was *the brainwashing device*! Her second thought was *all my gut reactions have gotten very strange...*

"All the hot water is gone."

Rae had no idea how so much hatred could be channeled into so few syllables. She opened her mouth to either laugh or scold her best friend for waking her with such a fright, but after a second look at Molly's face she thought better of it. "Well, that's...uh...a serious problem." She sat up carefully and pushed her messy curls from her eyes. The sounds and smells of breakfast were starting downstairs; already she could hear the hum of low voices and one high one she recognized as her mother's. Molly, however, was rooted in place.

"It *is* a serious problem," she hissed, waving what looked to be a loofah in the air. "Rae Kerrigan, how the hell am I supposed to prepare myself for a showdown with Jennifer Jones when I'm still sporting yesterday's leave-in conditioner?"

In moments like these, Rae never knew if she was kidding... Best not to risk it, though. Molly had developed a reputation for being rather...difficult in the mornings. "You're not," she said calmly, as she got out of bed and conjured herself a robe. She was getting quite good at it, she noted with absentminded pride. By the time her arms were in the air, the silk kimono was already sliding down over her.

Molly threw up her hands. "Well *obviously* I am, just because I didn't get up at like six in the morning like the rest of these maniacs to steal the first showers—"

"No, I mean, you're not going to fight Jennifer," Rae countered quickly, crossing to her window and throwing open the curtains, "I am. Me and Kraigan. That's it."

For a moment the shower situation was forgotten. But however impossibly, Molly looked even more dangerous than ever. "Oh yeah? And why is that?"

Rae sighed. She had been dreading this conversation since it first occurred to her late last night. There was simply no way on earth that she could ask her friends to go with her on this one. To them, Jennifer didn't pose an active threat. That, and she hadn't destroyed their lives. Not to mention, she was about as dangerous as a dragon on uppers.

No, for this fight only it was best that they stay behind.

"Molls, it's just way too risky for—"

The loofah hit her smack dab on the nose.

"Would you just give it a rest already? As if everything that we do together isn't that dangerous? As if you ever really had a choice as to whether or not Jules, Dev, and I were coming? I mean, we like to indulge you, sweetie, but come on—"

"I'm serious!" Rae exclaimed with sudden passion, as pressure she didn't know she was carrying came bursting forth. Molly frowned slightly at the look on her face and fell quiet. "This one isn't your fight. It's *my* fight. Jennifer took everything from me." Her voice started to shake with tempered hysterics. "Everything there was to take. And now—she's going to take something else. She's going to make me..." Her voice trailed off and she collapsed on the bed with her face in her hands.

A second later Molly joined her—rubbing a sympathetic hand on her back. "...a killer?" she guessed quietly.

Rae's shoulders shook as she considered the word. It couldn't be right, could it? 'Killers' were the kinds of bad guys the Privy Council used to send her and her friends after. They were just one step away from 'murderers.' Rae couldn't be *that*...could she?

Her dark hair fell between them as she hung her head. "I don't know if I can do it, Molls. I don't know if I can just go over there and kill her."

The two girls sat quietly for a while before Molly clapped her lightly on the shoulder. "And that's what makes you different from Kraigan."

Rae finally met her eyes, and Molly gave her a sad half-smile.

"You don't want to do it—but you know you have to do it *to keep your mother safe*." She emphasized the last part carefully, and Rae slowly nodded her head.

Molly was right. Jennifer Jones would never stop coming. It wasn't in her nature. If Rae wanted to keep her mother alive, she would have to take action first.

"So are we okay?" Molly asked gently.

For the first time in what felt like days, Rae's face relaxed into a sincere smile. "Yeah, we're okay."

Molly nodded curtly. "Good, because, not to make this day about me, but I wasn't at all kidding about that shower. Do you think you could conjure an extra water heater or something?"

Rae laughed and was about to answer when Beth called suddenly up the stairs. "Girls, get down here! Breakfast is getting cold."

Molly rolled her eyes and raced back to her room to get dressed, while Rae conjured herself a simple form-fitting outfit all in black. The same kinds of clothes she used in training and on missions. The same kinds of clothes Jennifer would most likely be wearing herself.

When she got downstairs, the four boys were already sitting around the table, gorging themselves on the morning banquet Beth had prepared. There was nothing but the sounds of forks scraping plates and the faint gurgling of the coffee maker as the kitchen flooded with the rich aroma.

For a moment Rae just leaned against the frame with a small smile, watching. She couldn't imagine a table of more drastically different personalities.

First there was Kraigan, sitting a little off by himself at the far corner—spearing a sausage on the end of what looked like a hunting knife. Crazy and lethal as they come. Then there was Julian, sitting a way off on his left. Quiet, but strong. A force all in his own right—with the kind of power that set him a step above the abilities at the table. Right by his side was Devon. Rae's heart automatically skipped a beat when she saw him. Handsome—devastatingly so—with enough latent ability to probably take down anyone seated around the kitchen. But humble. Kind. With twinkling eyes that Rae loved so much. And then, of course, at the end of the table was Gabriel...

Rae bit her lip pensively as she considered Gabriel. He wasn't her usual type that was for sure. In fact, he wasn't even the kind of guy who would usually be her friend. He was cocky, abrasive, annoying, infuriating—the list went on and on. To be frank, he was all the things that she loved Devon for *not* being.

And yet there was something special about Gabriel. Something that went beyond his stunning looks and scandalizing body. There was something deep in those sparkling green eyes...

"She's officially lost it," Kraigan declared abruptly. "I get her bacon."

Rae snapped back to attention to realize with acute embarrassment that all four boys were staring at her. Her cheeks flushed a deep pink as she ducked down her head and quickly joined her mother by the stove. "Uh...coffee?" she asked needlessly, just to change the subject.

Beth pursed her lips with a knowing smile, but handed her an empty mug and plate. "Eat up," she instructed seriously. "It's going to be a long day."

Rae specifically avoided the chair that Gabriel pushed out for her, and settled herself down beside Devon instead. "Morning," she said softly, sliding a piece of toast onto her plate.

"Morning yourself." He grinned, casting a quick look at Gabriel before kissing her on the cheek. All in all, he had been much better to Gabriel since he was nearly killed in London, but Gabriel was constantly doing things to set him off, and sometimes he simply couldn't resist returning the favor. "Was that Molly I heard screaming this morning? Something about showers?"

Rae chuckled. "Yeah, I suspect you're going to be hearing it in person before long."

"If it's anything like Peru, I'm out of here," Julian warned, shuddering with the dark memory. "In fact..." The fork slipped from his hand as his eyes turned white, scanning the immediate future for an encore of Molly's South American tantrum.

Kraigan watched him for a moment, fingers obviously itching to steal his ability and try for himself before he settled on stealing his bacon instead. "Why were you guys in Peru anyway? In fact, the four of you have been gone most of the summer. What gives?"

Gabriel took a swig of coffee before starting helpfully, "They were actually tracking down a list of tatùs before my old boss—"

"Could fine them for truancy," Devon finished quickly. "Gabriel worked in the admissions office at Guilder. Lots of disciplinary action, filing, that sort of thing."

Gabriel's eyebrows shot up over the rim of his coffee cup, but after glancing at Rae's stricken face he decided to let it go. "Yep, that's me. A virtual librarian." He grinned ironically. "That's how I got beat up."

Rae buried her face in her coffee as Kraigan cast each one of them a sour, disbelieving look. "Fine, don't tell me," he snapped. "Damn groupies. Hurry up and eat so that we can get to planning. I didn't track down that bitch for the last few months just so she could slip away while you guys feast on black pudding." Without another word he got up and stalked from the table, leaving the others in charged silence behind him.

When his footsteps had faded away, Gabriel turned to Devon with a wry grin. "Filing and disciplinary action? Yeah, I guess that's one way of putting it."

Rae snorted and set down her glass. "Sorry; you were so out of it yesterday we didn't really get a chance to fill you in on Kraigan."

"You mean your half-brother?" Gabriel grinned, and then looked speculative. "So he's the one I should be trying to charm if I want to eventually get with...you know..." He cocked his head towards Rae as Devon fumed in the background.

"He's also crazy." Rae ignored him, moving swiftly forward. "Certifiable. He's tried to kill me now a couple of times."

This time Gabriel's eyes flicked back to the hallway Kraigan had disappeared through, with a touch of that same protective instinct Rae had seen back at Guilder and a whole lot of rage. "Did he now?" he said the words calmly, but it looked as though he was half-ready to get up from the table and rip Kraigan limb from limb.

Rae shrugged casually, trying to cool him down. "My family's a little strange..."

Julian snorted. "Greatest understatement of the year."

"Not all of us are strange," Beth interjected sharply, tipping more bacon onto each of the boys' plates. "Just, well, most of us."

"Yeah," Devon agreed, flashing a mischievous grin. "Surely not the super-agent-turned- kidnap-victim who recently came back from the dead."

She swatted at him with a spatula, but laughed as she returned to the stove. Ever since their mysterious talk upstairs, the two seemed to have struck up an apparently unbreakable bond. A bond that Gabriel noted with the faintest hint of resentment as he returned to his coffee.

"So he's your crazy half-brother," he got them back on track. "What's the big deal?"

"He's also a sociopath who can touch you and steal your tatù," Julian warned darkly.

Devon's face turned grim. "And that's just one of his abilities..."

Gabriel glanced between them. "We covered that last night too. He's a hybrid. So what?"

Rae sighed softly. "I'm guessing Cromfield doesn't know about him, because he wasn't in any of his files... Jules and I checked."

"And one who can't know about Cromfield because we have no idea what the little bastard might do with that information or how it could come back and hurt Rae," Devon said sternly.

"Got it." Gabriel nodded briefly. Then he paused. "You know, you could have just asked me." The three of them shot him an almost nervous look and he chuckled. "I worked for him my whole life. Crom basically raised me. It's not like it's some big secret anymore," his eyes flickered to Beth. "You guys can talk about it. It's fine. It's the past and it's going to be something that helps me change my future."

Julian shifted uncomfortably. "Yeah, but he almost beat you to death and—"

"—and I'm here now," Gabriel finished steadily. "I want to help in any way that I can. And I certainly want to do everything in my power to keep Rae safe." He glanced pointedly at Devon before returning his eyes to Rae. "So just to set your mind at ease—no, Cromfield most definitely doesn't know about Kraigan. That's the kind of thing he would have told me." He grinned wickedly. "And would so love to know. He's going to kick his own ass when he finds out. Simon had a sweetie on the side?"

"Possibly more than one."

Rae swung around to look at her mother in surprise. "Excuse me?"

Beth shrugged. "If he had Kraigan, who's to say he didn't have more? I don't know. I obviously didn't know your father as well as I thought I did."

"None of us did."

"Cromfield didn't know that. He had no idea Simon had branched off in a... uh... new direction." Gabriel smiled at Beth. "He fooled a lot of people. He was smarter than Cromfield. I wish he had taken him down when he tried."

"What?" This was news to Rae, to all of them. "My dad tried to take Cromfield down?"

Gabriel waved his hand. "I don't know much. I was still a kid, but apparently Simon was as gung-ho about Cromfield as the Privy Council would like to believe."

"Interesting." Rae would love to ask him more questions, but now wasn't the time. They had to focus on Jennifer and also be aware that Kraigan might be listening in. Secrets were not something easy to keep anymore. Rae forced her shoulders to relax. "Thanks for sharing, Gabriel."

He winked and tapped his forehead. "You've got about twenty years of secrets from the other team's playbook up here. They're at your disposal."

It wasn't a particularly strange thing to say, but something about the way he murmured 'at your disposal' raised the hair on the back of her neck, and got Devon scowling. He was about to say something when the lights in the kitchen flickered, and the four of them raised their eyes to see Molly standing at the base of the stairs. Her hair hung in wet locks around her, and judging from the look on her face this was going to be much, much worse than Peru.

"I'm going to go...do something else," Julian muttered, getting to his feet and vanishing from the room quicker than anyone could stop him.

"Yeah, I'm," Devon pushed his plate back, "I think I'm done with breakfast." He quickly cleared his dishes and set them in the sink, squeezing Beth's shoulder as he walked past. "Thanks for cooking, Beth. It was delicious."

Rae's eyes narrowed as they followed the two of them out of the room. What on earth had happened there? When Beth first met Devon, she gave him absolute hell for dating Rae. Granted, she had been teasing, but the torture was real. And now?

"Well?!"

A chill ran down Rae's spine as she realized she had accidently allowed herself to be the only person left in the room with Molly.

"Um..." She got slowly to her feet, eyeing the sparks shooting from her friend's hand carefully, "Why don't I try conjuring that water heater...?"

Ten minutes later, everyone was dressed and dry (for the most part), and sitting around the living room as Kraigan stood in the middle.

"She's in a little town called Staffin on the western coast," he said authoritatively, obviously relishing the opportunity to grandstand. "Why, I don't know. But she's been there for the last two days without any indication of moving. It's a little seaside town, so it might be a little hard to sneak in undetected..."

Rae snorted. A *little* hard? That was a laugh. Even if Rae was invisible, Jennifer would be able to hear her coming from a mile away. Sneaking up on her would take a bit of creativity, to say the least.

"But it's a simple house, single story, with one way in and one way out. Once we get her in there, she's trapped." His mouth turned up in a chilling smile. "Then we can start to play..."

Beth rolled her eyes and leaned forward, tossing her hair back just like Rae did when she was impatient. "I'm afraid it's not going to be that simple, Kraigan. To start, I doubt there's a chance in hell that you'll make it within two miles of the house without her knowing. And once you're there, there's still the matter of *fighting* her."

Kraigan scoffed. "How hard could it be? I mean, really?"

Much to Rae's surprise, the eyes of the room turned to Gabriel instead of Beth. He had stayed very quiet during the entire meeting, glancing only once or twice at the map before leaning back in his chair, a troubled look clouding his handsome face.

It was only now that Rae realized why.

He had grown up with Jennifer, at least sporadically. In all likelihood she had been the one who actually helped raise him and Angel. Rae couldn't very well imagine Cromfield doing it. And now that Rae thought of it, the similarities between the two were startling.

"Jennifer trained you," she said softly, watching him until he finally met her eyes. His face tightened for a moment, and then he slowly nodded. Rae shook her head in disbelief, connecting a dozen dots that suddenly made perfect sense. "When you took down those two guards the night you broke me out of prison...I thought I'd never seen anyone fight like that. It was extraordinary; I didn't know how you did it. But I had seen someone fight like that before. Jennifer."

Both Devon and Kraigan had looked up with interest at the mention of these mythic fighting skills, but Gabriel was in his own little world.

For a brief moment all his usual cockiness went right out the window, and he looked shaky for the first time. "Since I was three," he said softly. "Me and Angie—she trained us up since we were three."

Angie? Rae frowned in confusion, before realizing. *Angel.* Gabriel still didn't know. There simply had been no time to tell him.

Sitting across the room, Julian's face had gone deathly pale. "Gabriel," he said tentatively, glancing at Rae to make sure it was okay, "Angel's not dead."

The room went dead quiet.

A muscle hardened in the back of Gabriel's jaw and he looked at Julian with a burning intensity that gave Rae the chills. "Say that again," he said quietly.

Julian's eyes softened sympathetically, almost apologetically, as he shook his head. "Rae didn't kill her. I could never have let that happen. I...I love her."

"I know that she loved you," Gabriel snapped. "It was all she ever talked about, in private, when..." his eyes flickered to Kraigan and he edited, "when no one else could hear."

Without even thinking about it, Rae reached over and took his hand. He looked completely overwhelmed, just barely holding it together. When he walked into the room, he thought he was about to lose whatever was left of his 'family' for good. Now he finds out that the girl, who for all intents and purposes was like his sister, was alive? "She's not dead," he said again, not as a question but more to reaffirm it for himself.

"No," Rae answered quietly, "she's most definitely alive. I'm so sorry we didn't tell you sooner... In our defense, we've only had about twelve hours with you when you weren't bleeding out." She laughed shortly and squeezed his hand. "But Angel's not dead. She's most definitely safe, and she's alive."

Kraigan threw up his hands impatiently. "I really don't see how this could matter less. Who the hell is Angel?"

"She's my—" both Julian and Gabriel started at the same time, before breaking off with a grin.

"She's my girlfriend," Julian finished.

"And she's...well, she's basically my sister. Who is very much alive," Gabriel added with a radiant grin that lit up his entire face.

Ironically enough, Rae saw Julian glance at Gabriel with a hint of that same 'brother-appeasing' supplication that Gabriel was looking at Kraigan with before he found out he was crazy.

Kraigan was unimpressed. "Okay, so why does that matter? And more importantly," his lips twitched as he looked Gabriel up and down but spoke to Rae, "*he's* your great fighter?" His eyes lingered on the sling supporting one of Gabriel's arms and the spattering of bruises and abrasions darkening his tan skin. "Please tell me that's a recent development."

Rae was about to answer, but Gabriel got to his feet with a small smile. Despite the fact that he was being physically held together by nothing greater than bandages and force of will, there was still an unmistakable aura that radiated out of him. He was not someone to be taken lightly. "You steal things, right? That's your thing?" he asked with that same little smile.

Rae shot Molly another secret grin and they settled back in their chairs to watch the magic unfold.

Kraigan was a force in his own right. There was no denying that. But to hear Gabriel reduce it down to petty theft? It was too priceless for words.

Kraigan's face turned a deep shade of red, but he stepped forward as well. "Amongst other things, yeah. And you— *bookkeeper*—how is it that dear little Rae thinks you walk on water?" He smirked at the look of horror that had abruptly transformed Rae's grin. "Or do you and Devon take turns now?"

Before anyone could say a word, both Kraigan and Gabriel flew suddenly backwards as a ball of molten fire crashed in between them. Rae ducked her head in fright, and then looked up to see her mother standing amongst the ashes of what used to be a recliner. The look on her face made Rae want to duck a second time.

"Do you want to ask that again, Kraigan?" she hissed softly.

For perhaps the first time in his life Kraigan bowed his head and took a step back.

"And do you want to answer it, Gabriel?"

Gabriel paled and shook his head, murmuring a respectful, "No, ma'am."

"Good." Beth's eyes narrowed. "Then suit up. It's time we dropped in on an old friend..."

Chapter 4

The hell that Molly, Devon, and Julian raised when they learned they were supposed to sit this one out could probably be heard all the way back in London. If it had been only Rae insisting, they probably would have just picked her up and carried her with them to the car. But none of them seemed particularly eager to go up against Beth, and when she told them to watch the house in case Jennifer showed up there instead, they complied without another word.

For his part, upon hearing the news Gabriel had stripped off his shirt and wandered casually to the bathroom, bravely volunteering to 'guard the tub.' He suffered no delusions that he was in any condition to fight, and while he was waiting to recover he had evidently decided to take pleasure in the finer things. Starting with what Molly complained was at least half of her coconut bath wash.

Rae also suspected that he didn't want to be anywhere in the vicinity when they finally tried to take Jennifer down. She could hardly blame him. Villain or not, the woman had helped take care of him as a boy. He wasn't stopping them, or warning her. That said a lot. And today it was enough.

"Take care of yourself, Rae," he murmured softly, tucking a stray curl behind her ear. He had yanked her suddenly into the bathroom as she was headed down to the car, and was watching her steadily as the room filled up with steam. "I don't have to tell you how dangerous she can be."

Rae appreciated the bluntness. It was far better than Molly's speech about 'how Rae Kerrigan was a champion and Jennifer had nothing on her.' It was even better than Devon's half-hearted request that she stay out of the line of fire and let Kraigan take the brunt of it.

It was honest. And it was true. Jennifer was bound to be one of the toughest opponents Rae had ever come up against. There was no point denying it. And there was no point avoiding it either. It was something she simply had to do...and try to survive.

"Thanks, Gabriel," she said a little awkwardly. Although it was no fault of her own she suddenly felt a bit guilty being locked away in a steamy room with him with his shirt off. "I should probably, uh, probably get going."

His eyes sparkled. "Yeah, you should."

Yet she found herself hesitating a moment longer. When he looked at her questioningly, she finally cleared her throat with a quick smile. "Any last advice?"

He grinned. "Jennifer's left-handed. She'll come at you from that side. Anticipate it, and you should be fine. As I recall you've got quite a bit of firepower to you. Use it." Hs face grew suddenly serious. "Use it—and come back."

A series of shivers ran up her arms, and she nodded quickly. Outside, the car horn honked twice. "I will. Thanks."

She was about to go when his hand shot out and caught her arm. When she turned around, all the playfulness was back and he was grinning again, cocking his head to the side as his blond hair spilled gracefully across his face.

"What? No kiss goodbye?"

She froze in place with her mouth half open. Was he serious? Then she remembered herself and narrowed her eyes with a glare. "You have no shame."

He chuckled and turned around back to the tub. "Nope. Not a bit."

Then he dropped his towel.

The drive to Staffin grew as quiet and uncomfortable as Rae thought possible. As they wound their way through the sprawling green hills, she couldn't help but wonder at the irony. If it hadn't been for Jennifer, and her adulterous father, how different this car ride could have been while being exactly the same.

Kraigan could have been Rae's full brother. They could have actually been in Scotland, living at their family house. Beth could have actually been driving them somewhere—to football practice or something else normal that didn't involve bloodshed and death.

In an alternate reality, this car ride could have been as normal as could be.

"Shit," Kraigan cursed, feeling around in his pockets, "I forgot my bigger knife."

Rae rolled her eyes and settled for looking out the window. Alternate reality was right.

They arrived at Staffin early in the afternoon, breezing through a crowded lot next to touristy pier selling seafood and kayak tickets. Since Jennifer would always be on her guard, but would be ready for a fight, the plan was relatively simple.

They would simply show up at her house, and pick a fight.

"It's just over the next bluff," Kraigan instructed once they were close enough. Like Rae, he was exhibiting the telltale jitters that inevitably came before such a moment. But while Rae's stomach was churning with both fear and dread, Kraigan had a manic smile on his face.

Beth parked in a clump of trees with an overhanging view of the house Kraigan had confirmed was Jennifer's. Although there was a chance she could have already heard them, Rae peered out the window curiously as she undid her safety belt. It was picturesque, nestled in the middle of a flowering garden with the sparkling blue waters of the ocean just beyond. There was nothing about it that indicated a cold-blooded murder lived inside. And yet here they sat, waiting.

"I'm going to check the perimeter, make sure we don't run into any surprises," Beth breathed, glancing about. "I'll be back in two minutes. Stay in the car until then, and when I get back we all go in together."

Both Rae and Kraigan nodded obediently as Beth slid out of the car. The second she was gone, Kraigan threw open his door and started heading straight down to the house.

"What the hell are you doing?" Rae hissed, using Jennifer's own tatù to dart out and catch him at top speed. "We're supposed to wait—"

"If you think I'm going to sit back and wait, you're even crazier than I am. But while you're here," he whirled around and grabbed her with a grin, "thanks for the tatù. It was the one I was hoping you'd use."

Rae's skin flushed hot then suddenly cold as Jennifer's prized leopard tatù was taken away from her. She clutched at her chest for a moment to steady herself, then shoved Kraigan as hard as she could.

"You bastard!" she hissed. "I'm trying to save your ass here. Give it back!" She knew he couldn't give it back, but she said it anyway. She couldn't possibly overestimate how much she would need that tatù. Although her body had slipped automatically into the next best thing; it was stronger and faster than Devon's—the only thing that would have put her on even footing if it came to hand-to-hand combat.

In an act of desperation she grabbed Kraigan's wrist, as if hoping the ability would flood back into her, but she was well aware it didn't work like that.

He yanked his arm away with a scoff. "I've been trying to stop myself from stealing it these last two days. And Julian's. Plus, your new lover's as well, but I had to keep the tracking ink I'd been using to hunt her down. Now that we're here that's no longer a problem."

"Actually..."

A new voice entered the conversation, and Kraigan and Rae whirled around to see Jennifer Jones standing in the grass behind them.

"...I'd have stuck with the tracking tatù." She looked exactly as Rae remembered: Long, wavy hair. Tight leather clothes that concealed the secret burns underneath. Piercing eyes that missed absolutely nothing.

Before Rae could get a good look, Jennifer was gone. Then Kraigan was gone too.

Acting more out of self-preservation than anything else, Rae switched from Devon's tatù to Cassidy's, melting invisibly away into the air. Without Jennifer's ink, she was at a clear disadvantage here. If the both of them could move faster than she could see, perhaps it was best if she couldn't be seen at all.

She certainly couldn't miss the sound of them, the resonances of two bodies colliding together again and again. There was the sharp cry of a woman, and then the lower one of a man. Rae watched and waited with bated breath, looking for even the slightest blur of color to indicate where they were.

When Kraigan cried out again, Rae saw them. Without stopping to think she dropped the cloak of invisibility and fired out a shockwave of Molly's electricity. Both of them went flying into the air before landing in sudden focus.

"Nice job, Kerrigan," Jennifer panted, wiping a small smear of blood from her lips with the back of her hand. "Just as I taught you to do. Except you do remember that you never beat me in a fight, right?"

Rae gritted her teeth. "Things change."

"And you," Jennifer glanced over at Kraigan, "I don't believe we've had the pleasure."

Although he had lasted longer than most anyone could, Kraigan was in much worse shape than Jennifer. He was bleeding from several large lacerations across his body, and one arm was sporadically twitching as if the muscle had been torn. While Rae had never seen him so discomposed, she'd never seen him so determined either.

"No," he murmured, leveling her with his gaze, "we haven't had the pleasure. I believe you met my mother. The day Simon Kerrigan was killed."

For a split second, Jennifer paused. Her eyes swept him up and down, taking in all the little details before her mouth turned up in an almost wistful smile.

"You do look a bit like Simon. I didn't realize before." Then her lips pulled back, revealing every one of her pearly teeth. "So you're the orphaned bastard he didn't want."

Faster than Rae could see, Kraigan reached into his coat and hurled a dagger straight at Jennifer's throat.

She deflected it with a simple flick of her wrist. "You may be his son, but you certainly don't have Simon's skill."

"We'll see about that—"

Rae wasn't about to let Kraigan get taken down in this fight, even if he did steal her greatest offensive weapon. Before her brother could charge again, Rae slipped in between them, battling Jennifer's ink with Devon's.

It was a rough fight. Devon may have been faster, but Jennifer's leopard had more strength. After taking just a few hits to the face, Rae felt as though she might black out. But all she needed was one moment, a single moment to switch from Devon's tatù to Angel's. Then they would see who had the upper hand.

"What's the matter, Rae?" Jennifer gasped as she kneed her in the ribs. "You're the one who showed up at my house, but I almost feel like your heart isn't really in this."

Touching Jennifer gave Rae her tatù back, but she didn't need it at the moment; she wanted Angel's. Rae spat out a mouthful of blood and leapt into the air, coming down on Jennifer's other side and kicking the back of her neck. She went flying forward but landed on her feet like a cat, launching herself at Rae before Angel's ink had time to take effect.

As Rae went skidding backwards, Kraigan leapt in for round two.

Except, he was so reckless he didn't stop to see that Jennifer had picked up his knife off the ground. He was so focused, he didn't even hear Rae scream.

"Kraigan—NO!"

But it was too late. The blur of colors suddenly ceased and the clearing was dead still.

Jennifer was standing behind Kraigan, using his body as a shield. One hand was holding a fistful of his hair and the other was pressing his own knife tightly against his throat.

Rae pulled herself slowly to her feet as all the blood drained from her face. Kraigan may be just a teenager, but Jennifer would not spare him. She would not be talked down, and she had no reason in the world to let him live. It would be very easy for her. And it would only take a second.

"Jennifer..." Rae tried again anyway, her mind racing for any trick she could use to set him free. "You don't want to—"

"Actually, I don't care much." Jennifer pressed the knife in tighter, and a thin trail of blood dripped down. "And seeing as how the second I let him go, the two of you are going to try to kill me again, I don't see why I—"

"Just do it, Rae," Kraigan growled, pale but determined. "Use your mother's fire—take us both down. It's the only way."

Rae's heart pounded in her chest as her eyes welled up with tears. On any given day, Kraigan might up and decide to try to kill her as well. His phrase from the day before flashed through her mind before she could stop it: *Kill two birds with one stone.* He posed a threat, just like Jennifer; he had from the day she met him. So why wouldn't she take this opportunity?

As her eyes locked on his murderous, bloody face, she set her jaw. Why? Because like it or not—and Rae didn't like it one bit—she was stopped by a single, undeniable truth.

Kraigan was family.

"DO IT!" he shouted again, straining a bit under the pressure of the knife. "FOR DAD!"

It was the first time Rae had ever heard him talk like that. Not his dad. Not the great Simon Kerrigan. Just *Dad*. Something that he and Rae shared.

"No," she said quietly. Then her eyes found Jennifer. "Take me instead."

Jennifer stared at her like she was crazy, while Kraigan's mouth fell open in utter shock.

For a second all was quiet, until Jennifer muttered, "You must be joking."

Unfortunately...no.

Rae pulled herself up to her full height, suddenly all business. "You know how many abilities I've collected over the years; you know exactly what I'm capable of. If you kill him now, I'll take you down in the process. You can be sure of that, but if you let him go you'll have a fair fight with me. And you already know that I've lost my best tatù."

Jennifer's lips twitched up into a smile, but Kraigan was staring at Rae like he'd never seen her before.

"I thought this was the boy who repeatedly tried to do you in, Kerrigan," she mocked, keeping the knife firmly in place. "He wants to kill you as much as he wants to kill me."

Rae sighed. "He's my brother. I'll chalk the rest up to sibling rivalry."

Jennifer laughed long and hard, then shoved Kraigan away from her with a sharp kick. He fell to the ground, holding his throat, trying to recover his senses as she beckoned Rae forward.

"Then let's have it, Rae. It's the way I would've preferred anyway. Just you and me. Like old times."

Jennifer and Rae lifted their hands and squatted, ready to pounce at the same time. Just as they did there was a streak of smoke, and Jennifer was suddenly lying on her back.

Bethany Kerrigan walked slowly out of the smoldering cloud, her fingers still dancing with the bright blue fire. "Oh but, Jenny, I'd rather have it be just you and *me*. Like old times."

Jennifer's face simultaneously flushed then paled as she saw Beth walking towards her. "I thought I'd heard another set of footsteps getting out of the car..." she murmured, "but then these two idiots showed up."

"Well," Beth flashed Kraigan and Rae a stern look, "they were told to wait."

It was incredible, to see a maternal flash when her hair was blowing around her in a cloud of smoke and flames. Despite being the most terrifying thing Rae had ever seen, her mother still managed to be *her mother*, no matter what she happened to be doing.

"Kids these days," she laughed lightly, before her face tightened with a mock frown. "Oh, I forgot, you wouldn't know anything about that, would you now, Jenny?"

Jennifer growled and flew towards her, but Beth sent her flying back on another wave of fire. The sickening smell of burnt leather and flesh filled the little clearing as Jennifer ripped off her jacket with a scream of pain.

"You stole her from me!" she shrieked. "MY daughter! MY chance to have a child. He didn't want to have her since he already had Rae!"

Beth's eyes flashed. "Something that had nothing to do with me, or Rae. And yet you felt the need to take away MY child. MY future with her. All for what? For *Simon*?"

"I LOVED HIM!" Jennifer screamed, tears and blood rolling down her face. "I loved him more than you ever did! More than you could ever love anyone!" she spat, her voice burning with anger. "You never understood love, Beth. You had that stupid adolescent love for Simon in your head. The one before he turned into who he was meant to be. You never could let that go."

"Oh Jenny," Beth shook her head, looking suddenly sad, "you're wrong again. See, I found a love deeper than anything you ever felt for Simon. A love you've never known. The love a mother has for her child." Her face grew hard. "A child that you tried to take away from me..."

Rae was hardly breathing. She'd inched her way over to Kraigan to make sure he was okay, but neither one of them could drag their eyes away from the two women. There was something horrifying about it, but something final. Like a chapter that had finally come to a close.

"Rae," Beth turned suddenly towards her, looking as calm and peaceful as when they were back on the farm with Molly training to hit that far tree, "*get down.*"

Rae barely had time to pull Kraigan with her to the ground before the wave of molten fire crashed over their heads. There was time enough for Jennifer to scream. One final pitiful sound.

Then all was quiet.

Chapter 5

Rae walked up the front steps to her mother's house, clutching the smoldering remains of Jennifer's leather jacket. It was all that remained of her. The only thing that survived the blast.

And, while Rae didn't know why, she felt the need to keep it.

The door pulled open before she could even touch it. Julian was standing on the other side. One look at his face and Rae knew that he'd seen everything. Without saying a word he pulled her into his long arms, squeezing her tightly before stepping back to allow the three of them inside.

Neither Beth, nor Kraigan, nor Rae had said a single word on the way home. It seemed as though there was nothing left to say. Jennifer was dead. They were alive. It was over.

The other three were frozen in various states of waiting in the kitchen. Julian must have told them what had happened. The second Rae walked through the door Devon leapt to his feet and crossed the kitchen in three long strides. She was in his arms the next second. His racing heart began to slow as he held her against him, and she felt his chest relax in a long, worried sigh.

Gabriel had also peeled himself away from the wall when she walked in, but when he saw Devon and her embrace he casually reassumed his original position, as if he hadn't moved in the first place.

"So," Molly murmured, giving Rae's hand a quick squeeze, "Julian told us. We pulled out some bandages and gauze and stuff for Kraigan. It's in the bathroom upstairs."

Devon pulled back and looked Rae up and down in sudden concern. "Sweetheart, you're bleeding."

Rae glanced down in surprise, seeing the steady red drip onto her coat. The gashes from where Jennifer had kicked her in the face still hadn't healed, and, in spite of her ability to heal herself, for some reason her body hadn't switched into Charles' tatù.

"I don't..." her voice trailed off as her fingers came up to her face, "I didn't realize..."

"That's okay," Devon's fingers closed around hers before he brought them to his lips, "you were probably in shock. Your body didn't switch over. We can get you cleaned up upstairs. Right after Kraigan—"

Kraigan shoved past him in that moment and stalked away up the hall. The gang stared after him in wonder, but Rae merely sighed. Although she hadn't meant to at the time, it seemed she had fundamentally altered things when she volunteered to take Kraigan's place. Now there was no going back, and Rae wouldn't have even if she could. Now all that was left to do was wait and let the chips fall where they may.

"Let's go upstairs. Let me take care of that," Devon said softly, brushing her hair back to get a better look at the abrasions on her face.

Rae nodded robotically before glancing suddenly behind her. "Mom?"

Shouldn't they say something? Talk about what happened? Jennifer was *dead*. How could they just carry on with their night like nothing had happened?

Beth looked tired—three decades'-worth of tired—but she still managed a small smile. "Go upstairs, honey. Devon will sort you out. We can...we can work it out in the morning."

Rae nodded again and headed mechanically down the hall. On the way past him, Gabriel caught her eye. For all the things he might have been feeling, his expression was truly unreadable. A million unspoken things were dancing behind his eyes as they locked onto hers, but before she could even register what was happening she was up the stairs.

Devon locked the door to the bathroom behind them and sat her down gently on the counter. He reached automatically for the bottle of rubbing alcohol left out for Kraigan, before remembering himself with a small smile.

"Do you want me to? Or would you rather use Charles' tatù?"

Instead of answering, Rae closed her eyes and felt as the familiar ability floated to the surface of her skin. There was a warm sort of buzzing, and the next thing she knew the stinging pain in her face was all but gone. All that remained now was a dull ache that radiated through her entire body.

One that she didn't think had anything to do with the beating she'd taken.

When she finally looked up, she realized that Devon's eyes were locked on the jacket she was still clutching to her chest. It was stained with her blood now as well as Jennifer's. At least, in the places it hadn't been burned clean through with Beth's vengeful fire.

He didn't ask her why she kept it, and for that Rae was grateful. He simply eased it from her fingers and set it on the counter before starting up the shower. As he did so, a tiny glass bottle slid out of the jacket pocket and fell upon the floor.

They both looked at it in surprise, astonished that it was there and that it hadn't broken or melted with the fire.

Devon knelt down and held it up between careful fingers. There was scribbled writing in permanent marker on the side, and he squinted as he tried to make it out.

"I think this..." His eyes widened in wonder. "Rae, I think this is a bottle of the serum Cromfield's been working on."

She stared at him for a long time before staring down at the bottle.

"Sample 3V421," he read off the side, "with extraction 'A.'" He paused for a moment, thinking, before he said, "Didn't Angel say that the latest batches were infused with samples of her blood to be used as a paralytic?"

"I don't..." Rae simply shook her head and covered her face. This day needed to end. It had gone on long enough and she didn't have it in her tonight to answer any of these questions.

"I'm sorry," Devon said softly, setting down the bottle on the counter and drawing her back into his arms. "It doesn't matter right now. All that matters is you're safe. You all are."

Rae pressed her face against his chest, breathing in the steam with short ragged, gasps. "Not Jennifer."

Again she felt him sigh.

"No, not Jennifer." He kissed the top of her head. "Life doesn't always make sense, and the heart doesn't always understand what the head realizes."

Considering the showers Rae and Devon had shared in the past, this one wasn't even remotely romantic. She had stood perfectly still as he helped her undress—slipping off his own clothes without a word as he joined her under the warm water. Then, with the gentlest hands she could imagine, he began slowly rubbing her clean.

Little streams of caked-on blood poured off of her and ran down the drain as he passed over them with a soft washcloth. He poured a dash of lavender shampoo onto her scalp and began slowly working it through with his fingers, taking care to keep the suds from her eyes. When he was finished he kissed her forehead, wrapped her up in a towel, and carried her off to bed.

Get it together, Rae. You're acting like a child, she thought as he tucked her tightly beneath the covers before slipping under himself. *I* am *a child!!* her inner self screamed.

Rae couldn't get it together. She wasn't sure she ever would after today. She wasn't remotely okay. She had seen things today, things that somehow topped her list of crazy things that had happened to her. Or maybe it was an accumulation of everything, from the fire as a child, the abduction and betrayal from Lanford... the list just went on and on.

Ever since she'd gone to Guilder and realized what she was, realized what her name implied, she had been fighting against a clear enemy. Fighting evil on the side of good.

But this? Jennifer? Her mentor and her mother's former best friend?

How was she supposed to be okay with this? How was she supposed to be okay with any of it? The simple answer: she wasn't. At least not tonight.

With a broken sigh she turned on her side and curled up beneath Devon's arm, resting her cheek against the smooth skin on his chest.

She simply couldn't handle any more drama tonight...

"Why the hell did you do that?!"

Rae jerked awake with a gasp as the light suddenly snapped on. The sky outside was still dark but that didn't seem to matter to Kraigan, who was standing in the door frame with his arms folded angrily over his chest.

His glare only intensified as she bolted upright and pulled the sheets up to her chin.

Tatùs flipped through her at a dizzying pace, trying to decide which one would be the most effective. Her body didn't seem to know what Kraigan was after. "Kraigan, what are you—"

"What the hell did you think you were doing?!"

In all the time they'd spent battling each other, she had never seen him so angry. He was literally beside himself.

Devon threw a protective arm around her, his eyes flashing while simultaneously holding the sheets securely at his own waist. "Kraigan, I don't know what the hell you think you're doing, but you need to get the hell out of here right now!"

"YOU HAD NO RIGHT!"

For a moment, both Rae and Devon fell into stunned silence, just watching in shock as Kraigan lost the composure that reminded her so much of her father.

"YOU HAD NO RIGHT SAYING THAT TO HER!"

"Who? What?" Devon looked at Rae in complete bewilderment. "What's he talking about? What the hell's going on?"

Rae simply stared at her brother, unable to look away. "I offered to take his place," she said quietly. A small part of her was surprised that Julian had failed to report this. She assumed it was for her benefit. There was no way Devon was going to take it well. "Jennifer was about to kill him and I did the only thing I could think to protect him. I offered to take his place."

Right on cue Devon paled in rage. He made as if to stand up before remembering he was naked, and hastily clutched the sheets around his waist. "Why the hell would you do that?" he yelled, echoing Kraigan's exact words without seeming to realize it.

Rae blushed, but kept her eyes on Kraigan. "You're my little brother."

Kraigan shook his head back and forth so fast it was like he was using a tatù. "No, you can't pull that shit on me now. Not after everything that's happened—"

"Everything you made happen," Rae countered evenly. "I never wanted any of that. I never wanted to hurt you, Kraigan. Like it or not, you're family."

"STOP SAYING THAT!" His skin had gone bone-white and his hands were trembling. It seemed the great Kraigan had finally met his match. But it wasn't by any enemy of his own design. He had been beaten by something greater, something he didn't understand. Something that was tearing him apart. "Why did you have to..." Actual tears flew angrily off his face, and he stared at Rae like he actually wanted to kill her. "You can't just...you ruined..." He struggled to catch his breath. "You had NO RIGHT to do that!"

Before Rae could answer, the door behind him pushed open and Kraigan fell forward a step, turning around with a glare as a head of shaggy blond hair stuck itself into the room.

"Hey guys, having a midnight get-together without me?" Gabriel asked cheerfully. His eyes travelled from Rae and Devon's stricken positions over to where Kraigan looked like he might be contemplating jumping out the window. His eyes slid back to Rae and started at her feet under the thin sheet, up to her chest where she was clutching the sheet. "Kinky threesome..." he murmured. "You guys might hate each other, but you do realize that you're still technically related, right?"

"Get the hell out of here, Gabriel!" Devon shouted. "Both of you!"

Rae wrapped the sheet around her like a dress and flushed beet red, wishing very much that the ground would open up and swallow her whole.

"But I just got here," Gabriel said with that same impish grin, perching on the edge of the bed just far enough away that Devon would have to release the shared sheet if he wanted to try to expel him by force. Something Gabriel was obviously banking Devon would not be willing to do. "Anyway, what're we talking about? The yelling's half muffled by these old walls."

"What are you *doing* here, Gabriel?" Rae asked tensely, trying to pull herself together while making sure that everything important was still covered.

Gabriel's eyes lingered a moment on her flushed skin and bare shoulders, before he flashed a casual smile. "I was just coming in to check on you after the night you had." His gaze flicked quickly to Devon as his tone soured. "I didn't know you had company."

Devon's chest rose and fell with quick, shallow breaths as his fingers tightened in rage. "Why the hell wouldn't she? I'm her damn *boyfriend*, Gabriel—get it through your head! She's with me!"

In spite of the look of lethal promise on Devon's face, Gabriel stayed perfectly composed. "I only meant that I was under the impression the two of you weren't allowed to...*visit* while under Beth's roof. I wonder what she would think about it..."

"Oh come on, like you're really going to tell her," Rae hissed.

"No honey," he reached across the bed and squeezed her ankle under the sheet, "I'd never do that to you."

"That's it!" Devon finally stood up, taking his half of the sheet with him. "Get out!"

Rae yelped and struggled to keep herself covered as Gabriel stood up with a chuckle. "Nice ink, man. I've never really seen it up close."

Devon clenched his jaw. "I'm going to count to three and if you're not out of this room, I don't care how hurt you are, I swear I'm going to tear you to pieces."

"I can't believe you did that," Kraigan muttered from the corner. He was still looping on his same, desperate argument; the only one completely oblivious to the boys' fight. "I would never have done that for you."

For the first time, Rae cocked her head to the side and rose to the bait. "Really? You would have just let her kill me?"

He turned back to her with a scowl. "It would have saved *me* the trouble, so yeah."

"Oh, you are so freaking unbelievable—"

But the second Kraigan said his words, the two other boys seemed to have forgotten about each other entirely and they both turned to Kraigan in a rage.

"Say that again," Devon threatened, leveling him with his eyes. "I don't care what tatù you may be carrying at the time. Probably Jennifer's, but mark my words; Rae might not be able to do you in herself, but she's a better person than I am. If you threaten her even one more time I'm going to throw you out the window. We'll see if you can survive that."

"If you can," Gabriel took over, rising up from the mattress and folding his arms as he positioned himself in front of Rae, "then I'll come down there and you can see how they train bookkeepers to fight nowadays in person. I promise, it won't be something you friggin' like."

Kraigan's eyes flashed and he flew forward, bringing them toe to toe. "Coming from the guy who looks like he's been fed through a wood-chipper? Yeah, I have to say I like my odds—"

"I'd take that bet." Rae hung her head in dismay as Julian suddenly slipped inside. He was wearing nothing but a pair of low-hanging pants and a smile as he glanced around the room. "I've been watching from my room for the last ten minutes to see how this played out, but then I realized I could just watch it all in person!"

"Great," Rae muttered, still hiding her face, "now it's a freakin' party."

"Conjure us some popcorn," Julian instructed, taking a seat on the bed beside her. It was only then that he glanced down in surprise. "Rae, you do realize you're not wearing anything, right?"

Her eyes snapped shut as she struggled to rein in her temper. "Yeah, I'm pretty clear on that Jules, thanks."

"Could everyone just GET THE HELL OUT?!" Devon commanded.

"Not until she and I straighten this out!" Kraigan cried.

"And not until I get at least a glimpse of what's beneath those sheets..." Gabriel gave Rae a seductive wink.

"That's it!" Devon roared, pacing forward in a makeshift sarong, "I warned you!"

"Dude," Julian looked scandalized, "why is everyone naked?!"

However, before anyone could come to actual blows, the door banged open again.

"What on earth is going on in here?"

The conversations flying around the room came to a temporary stop as Molly walked inside, throwing the door shut behind her. She blinked around in disorientation for a second, her eyes resting on each of the frozen men before her eyes came to rest on Rae.

In moments such as these, a good best friend would know what to do simply by the look of panic in her friend's eyes. Considering the level of chaos in the room, Rae slipped into Maria's telepathy, just in case.

Molly, get me the hell out of here!

Molly's eyes grew wide and she nodded slowly. Then she turned to the guys with a look so lethal, it had no place on the face of a mere stylist.

"I'm going to say this one time, and one time only. You will all stop this nonsense at once. You will not speak. You will not argue. You will not move. You will avert your eyes until Rae has left the room." She rolled her eyes. "Then you can all go on killing each other."

Kraigan gritted his teeth as he towered threateningly over the little redhead. "She and I aren't finished talking yet—"

There was a flash of blue light, and Kraigan was sliding slowly down the far wall. One arm reached out to steady himself as he pulled himself up with a gasp.

Molly smiled coldly. "I think you are."

Much to Rae's secret glee, Kraigan immediately edged out of the room, casting Molly a terrified glance as he did so—his left arm twitching uncontrollably.

Once he was gone, Molly turned to the others. "Anyone else?"

"Molly Skye," Gabriel raised his eyebrows in approval, "I didn't know you had it in you."

Her eyes flashed with the same blue energy. "Oh...just give me a reason, blondie."

He sobered up quickly and fell silent with the rest of them, waiting for Rae to take her leave.

But Rae was staring at Molly in silent panic. Under the thin sheet she was completely naked. How on earth was she supposed to just leave?

Molly caught her stare and closed her eyes with a look of strained patience. "You're a super-hero, Rae. Figure it out..."

With a sudden jolt of illumination, Rae's cheeks flushed. "Oh." Then she melted away invisibly into the air.

Molly shook her head. "There you go."

Rae slowly untangled herself from the mess of sheets, trying to ignore it as the boys watched with varying degrees of fascination, and extracted herself from the bed, getting hesitantly to her feet.

It felt utterly bizarre to walk past Devon, Gabriel, and Julian while completely naked. Like that nightmare you have of showing up at school without your clothes.

She rushed quickly past them, careful not to touch anyone, before coming to stop at Molly's side. They were all still staring aimlessly around. Only Devon with his heightened hearing had followed every movement, though he couldn't see her doing them. He stared at the air where she stood now, offering her a sad half-smile—a silent apology for the way the night had to end.

Invisible to the world, Rae smiled back. Then her eyes drifted to Gabriel, who happened to be staring in the right place as well, and she shivered. *Time to get the hell out of here.*

She tapped Molly on the shoulder, and Molly jumped a mile.

"*Goodness*! That's so icky-creepy," she murmured before opening up the door and gesturing to her own room up the hall.

Rae tiptoed away at the speed of light but she could still hear perfectly as Molly stuck her head back into the room with what was sure to be a wide grin.

"Try not to kill each other, I guess. Or not."

Rae could almost hear the shrug of her best friend's shoulders.

"Saves me the hassle."

Chapter 6

Maybe it was the fact that Rae's best friend had asked her to make popcorn when she wasn't wearing any clothes. Or maybe it was that her boyfriend tried to kill her brother whilst wearing a blanket sarong. Or that Gabriel had stared, straight on, at her invisible naked body.

Rae wasn't able to sleep that night.

Under the cover of Molly's loud, triumphant snoring, Rae conjured herself a thick fleece trench coat and crept out the open window. Despite the older design of the house, the lock on the window had been oiled down, even shaved a bit so it wouldn't make any noise.

Maybe my mother did this, she thought to herself as she perched on the roof and gazed up at the moon. *Maybe this window was her childhood escape hatch. Maybe it could have been mine...*

She sighed deeply and laid her head back against the chilled tile plates. For once, the house beneath her was at peace. All the explosive personalities were finally locked away in their separate corners, either dreaming already or searching for sleep. The only sound, save for the wind, was the soft hooting of a tawny owl as it went about its nighttime hunt.

Slipping into Devon's tatù, she located the bird quickly and thoughtfully followed along as its tiny wings angled towards the barn. Then she frowned.

There was a tiny light flickering in the far window, something so faint that she most likely wouldn't have been able to see it if it wasn't for the help of her ink.

Dropping noiselessly to the ground, she gathered her coat tighter around her and flitted across the damp ground to the huge oak door. It was slightly ajar, and she was able to slip through the crack without disturbing it in the slightest. Once she was inside, she looked around and gazed up at the high ceilings with a bit of trepidation.

The first time she'd ever come in here she'd been in temporary awe. It was just so massive and...well, alone. A place of complete and utter isolation. Part of her craved to stay there forever.

She shivered now. There was something else about the barn that had set her on edge from the moment she stepped inside. There was a history to this place. It was the beginning of something. Something that might have started innocently enough, but Rae had the feeling they were still sorting out the repercussions of it today.

She drifted along, following the flickers of the distant light as it reflected off the rafters until she rounded a corner and saw her mother. Beth was sitting on a long bench pushed up against the far wall of the barn, a little candle by her side. Rae knew instantly what the spot represented. A tatù snuck its way over and seemed to whisper the truth in her ear. It was the same bench where her mother and father had shared their first kiss. Had fallen in love. Had started this whole mess in the first place.

"Hey," Rae said softly, not wanting to startle her.

Beth jumped anyway, but smiled when she saw her daughter. Without saying another word she patted the bench beside her, and Rae took a seat. They were quiet for a long time, each listening to the gentle midnight breeze as it slithered in and out of the rafters.

"The house we were at today..." Beth began softly, staring uncertainly at the sky, "Simon bought Jennifer that house."

Rae's heart skipped a beat. "He did? How do you know that?"

"I called the town realtor and looked up the records," Beth admitted, pushing back her long hair and looking suddenly tired. "I couldn't help it. I'd a hunch and I had to know."

Rae took a silent minute to absorb this. "So when Jennifer went to Scotland...she might not have been coming after us after all?"

"She might have just been going home." There was another pause and Beth looked at Rae sharply. "Don't get me wrong. Jennifer was still and would always be working for Cromfield. She was a threat who had to be eliminated," she said with absolute certainty, and in spite of herself Rae began to relax. When Beth was finished speaking, her eyes clouded once more. "But, yes...she might have just been going home."

"I don't understand," Rae said with a trace of anger, "why would Dad—I mean, *Simon*—buy her a house in Scotland? Just a few hours away from this one?"

"Simon always loved it here," Beth answered quietly, her eyes a million miles away. "It was one of the only things I can say for certain that he did love."

"Mom..." Rae took her hand, suddenly struck to the core with how sad it must be for her mother to come back here. To sleep in this house, to sit on this bench. "He loved you. I know he did."

Beth smiled softly, patting her fingers. "You don't need to reassure me of that. Simon was a difficult man. He certainly didn't make it easy to love him, and love didn't come easy to him. But once it did...it was a thing that was nearly impossible to shake."

Rae's face fell. "Jennifer certainly couldn't shake it."

"Well, we can't always choose who we love." Beth shot Rae a sideways smile. "A lesson I think you're starting to figure out, my dear."

Rae's cheeks burned, and she hoped her mother couldn't see it in the dim candle light. "You heard, didn't you? I hoped you were too far away..."

"Honey, people in London heard that."

Great. Rae tucked her hair behind her ears and gazed in the direction of the house. Although it pained her to say it she suspected her mother wasn't just talking about the explosive nature of the confrontation, but of one or two specific people involved. She rolled her eyes when Beth chuckled at her hesitation, and sighed. How was she supposed to talk to her mother about what was going on when she didn't understand it herself?

Devon or Gabriel? Gabriel or Devon?

Damn! When had that become a question?

It wasn't really a choice. She was with Devon. She loved Devon. With all her heart.

It's just, Gabriel made her feel...*alive.* Uninhibited. Free. Like a blank canvas. Untouched by the dangers of her past or the limits of her name.

An older, wiser part of her understood the reasons for that. Gabriel simply hadn't been there during all the turmoil of the previous years like Devon was. He hadn't had to wade through the muck with her, keeping her head above water. It was easy to look at him and see a simple, trouble-free life.

Except that a simple, trouble-free life wasn't real. And Devon shouldn't be penalized for being present when she'd needed him the most. On the contrary, it was one of the reasons she loved him so much. Because he loved her unconditionally. Despite her darkness, despite her name. He'd give up anything and everything for her, and she knew it.

But, in a way, that was just another reason that she liked Gabriel. She knew it, even if she didn't want to admit it to herself.

There was a weight to that—a responsibility that came with the unconditional affection of Devon. One that, while being 'the thing' that people spent their whole lives searching for, she sometimes worried she just wasn't ready for as a teenager.

Yet there was no pressure with Gabriel. No weight, no expectation. Just lightness. An effervescence that he seemed to radiate to everyone around him. To everyone in reach of his light.

"I'm sorry," Beth squeezed her hand suddenly, "I didn't mean to make you fret."

"You didn't," Rae assured her quickly but her heart wasn't in it. Strangely enough it wasn't the Devon-Gabriel conflict that most troubled her about what happened that night.

It was her brother.

"I don't know what to say to Kraigan," she murmured, hugging her knees to her chest. "You should have seen the look on his face tonight. He was so...*betrayed*, somehow. And I don't understand it. All I did was try to help—"

"I know you did and so does he. But it's not as simple as all that." Beth squeezed her hand again. "Kraigan needed to hate you, sweetie. You got the life he thinks he wanted. The father he thought he wanted. The ability he always wanted. And then, as it turns out, *your* mother is still alive. When you offered to give yourself up for him...I think it made hating you pretty hard."

Rae shook her head miserably. "Well, he's still managed it. Trust me."

"I don't think he hates you as much as you might think. Quite the opposite." Beth smiled warmly at her and helped her to her feet. "Shall we head inside? It's getting cold."

"Yeah." Rae cast a final look around the barn, and a familiar chill ran down the back of her neck. She shook it off quickly and joined her mother by the door. They'd better get some rest if they wanted to survive the gang at breakfast tomorrow. If tonight was any indication, it was going to be rough.

"So then I threw him down one of those ventilation ducts and headed back to the villa. To be honest, the hardest part of the whole thing was scrubbing off all that liquid latex..."

Rae froze in the doorframe on her way into the kitchen the next morning. She couldn't have heard that right, could she?

Much to her utter astonishment, Kraigan and Gabriel were in the middle of an animated conversation over eggs and toast, practically grinning as they told each other tale after tale. Julian was sipping an espresso in the corner, looking dubious, but even he couldn't hide his amusement.

"What about Roberto?" Kraigan asked excitedly.

Gabriel downed his coffee with an unconcerned shrug. "He turned up in a duck pond about a week later. Said he couldn't be called upon to testify because he was color-blind."

Kraigan roared with laughter, and Rae's mouth fell wide open.

Kraigan...*laughing*? A non-sinister, non-supervillain laugh? She didn't even know he could do that. It sounded incredibly out of place coming from his mouth.

"Sis!" he cried, spotting her. "Stop lurking about and pull up a chair." He yanked out the one beside him and Rae eyed it like it might explode.

"I'm sorry. I think I just stepped into a parallel universe." She glanced at Julian for help, but he just shrugged over his coffee.

Gabriel, however, leapt to his feet and led her graciously to a chair; pulling it out and pushing it back in behind her. "Toast?" he offered with a smile.

"Uh...yeah. That would be great."

As he tipped some onto her place, her eyes flickered again to Kraigan. He didn't appear to be armed; in fact, the only thing he seemed to be interested in was helping himself to more potatoes.

Nevertheless, she switched into Molly's tatù and kept her fingers at the ready. "So, uh...looks like everyone's in a pretty good mood today," she said tentatively, her eyes flashing to Gabriel for explanation.

He smiled again. "Yeah, well, after you bolted naked from the room last night, I decided to go and make peace with your brother over there."

Rae blinked. "You did?"

"Of course!" He clapped Kraigan on the shoulder, and to Rae's continued bewilderment Kraigan actually flashed him a grin. "As it turns out, there's far more that unites us than divides us."

In spite of herself, Rae couldn't help but laugh. "So that's all you two did? You just found some common ground?"

"More like...a common enemy." Gabriel winked.

Ironically, at that precise moment Devon walked through the door.

Rae's heart dropped to her stomach and she sank down in her chair. "Oh...I see."

"Morning," Devon kissed her on the cheek and pulled up a chair beside her, nodding at Julian but ignoring the other two entirely. "Sleep alright?"

Rae couldn't stop glancing between her brother and the eternal thorn in her side, already dreading the unholy alliance that had sprung up between them. "Good enough—when I finally got to sleep."

"On that note," Kraigan turned to Rae with a good-natured sternness, "I know that we've got some time to make up in terms of sibling bonding, but I have to say I think it's entirely inappropriate that you were planning on sharing a bed with Devon last night."

Julian snorted coffee through his nose and quickly excused himself, while Devon looked at Kraigan in shock.

"Entirely...inappropriate?" he echoed, not understanding what was going on.

Kraigan's eyes narrowed as he sneered. "Well, I was going to say *nauseating*, but I didn't want to spoil a family breakfast by recalling images of you wrapped in a sheet about to do my sister."

Rae's head sank into her hands. "Waking up this morning was a mistake..."

"Nonsense," Gabriel declared, enjoying himself immensely. "Here, take a biscuit." He tossed one onto her plate and leaned back to enjoy the mayhem he'd spent the night engineering.

"I don't..." For the first time, Devon looked a bit uncertain. His eyes flashed between Gabriel and Kraigan as he tried to discern their new shift in dynamics. Coming up blank, he turned again to Kraigan. "What the hell are you talking about? Since when do you give a damn what happens to Rae or who she happens to—"

"To *have sex with*?" Kraigan banged his hand on the table, though his eyes were dancing. He was obviously enjoying himself just as much as Gabriel was. "Maybe that's not a big deal to you, Wardell, but in this house—"

"*In this house?!*" Devon cut him off, staring at him like he'd gone crazy. "You do realize this isn't *your* house right? That Beth's not really your family?"

Kraigan got to his feet with all the self-righteous indignation of an Amish minister. "I am not going to sit idly by and allow you to tarnish my sister's—my—good name, just for the sake of satisfying your debauched urges."

Devon's mouth fell open as Rae turned to Gabriel with a glare. "Gabriel," she lowered her voice to a hiss, "what the hell have you done?"

Gabriel bit his lip to stop from laughing, watching as Devon tried to half-heartedly defend himself. Gabriel shook his head. "Oh, come on, it's not like he's wearing a 'Team Gabriel' tee-shirt." He dropped his voice conspiratorially. "Although, I'm not above asking you to conjure one—"

"Gabriel!"

"We needed a truce, didn't we?" he murmured quietly. "You needed something to re-direct him so he didn't turn all that frustration onto you." He glanced at the heated argument raging on between Devon and Kraigan with a smile. "I merely re-directed him."

While Rae couldn't help but admire the wisdom in this tactic, it was Gabriel's specific strategy that was giving her heartburn. "So you had to re-direct him onto—"

"Honey?" He cocked his head to the side with a sweet smile.

"What—?" Her cheeks flamed red. "*Don't* call me that!"

"Rae," he rolled his eyes and shoved forward a little jar, "I meant for your biscuit." His eyes sparkled as he spooned her out a dollop. "Honestly, don't be so narcissistic."

She dropped her head to the table with a groan. "This cannot be happening again."

"Hey," he nudged her sympathetically, "at least you're not naked this time... Unfortunately for me." She was about to retort when he leaned in with a sudden, curious frown. "Actually, on that note, I was going to ask: Do you and Devon ever...you know...when he can't see you—"

Pushed past her limit, Rae leapt to her feet with an infuriated cry. "I am NOT going to sit here with you and discuss my SEX life over BISCUITS! And FREAKIN' HONEY!!"

The whole table went dead quiet.

Strangely enough their eyes weren't fixed on her. They were fixed on something behind her. She was about to turn around when a low voice boomed out over the room.

"Well, that *is* a relief."

Rae's eyes snapped shut as absolute mortification threatened to swallow her whole. *Really? Could this get any worse?*

"Nice to see you again, Miss Kerrigan," Carter continued with a wry smile in his voice. "I trust you've been keeping busy..."

The arrival of the President of the Privy Council prompted several things to happen at once. To start, both Gabriel and

Kraigan suddenly made themselves quite scarce. Kraigan had been near the top of the PC's most wanted list for some time, and Gabriel had just confessed to being a spy. Needless to say, they both suddenly 'lost their appetites' and vanished outside. But as both boys magically disappeared upon Carter's arrival, Beth just as suddenly materialized. The second she heard Carter's voice, she went tearing into the kitchen and threw herself into his arms.

"James!" she gasped, pulling back for a kiss. "I thought it was you!"

"You're lucky it was," he smiled, a relaxed, happy smile that seemed just as out of place on his face as Kraigan's laughter was just moments before. "I'd certainly hope that you wouldn't greet just any man who walked into your kitchen this way."

"Awkward," Rae murmured under her breath, sinking back into her chair at the table.

Carter raised his eyebrows. "You want to talk about *awkward* right now?"

Rae ignored her mother's look of confusion and buried her face in her biscuit. "No."

"So, why are you here, James?" Beth asked, glancing nervously outside. "You better have come alone. If I see even a single guard—"

"I came alone," he said quickly, holding up his hands to calm her. "I'd have come even sooner, but your daughter caused a bit of an uproar when she left Guilder."

Rae shrugged indifferently under their joint stares. "I would've thought I made everything much simpler for the Council by leaving." There was a lot more she wanted to say but bit her lip instead.

"*Simpler,*" Carter laughed under his breath. "Well you certainly made a splash, I'll give you that. You've inspired the Privy Council to do something it hasn't done in over five hundred years."

Beth folded her arms anxiously across her chest as Rae slowly set down her biscuit. "And what's that?"

A feeling of dread stirred in the pit of Rae's stomach.

Carter gave her a hard smile.

"They've elected a second president."

Chapter 7

"Please say it's me."

Carter and Beth turned to Rae in a single movement. While her mother appeared confused, Carter had ice in his veins.

"I'm sorry, honey," Beth shook her head, "but, pardon?"

"The second president," Rae clarified innocently. "Please tell me that after I left they took a secret vote and it's actually me." Carter opened up his mouth to cut in, but before he could say a word Rae slammed her hand down on the table. "I vote to disband!"

"Rae Kerrigan!" Beth exclaimed, casting an apologetic look at Carter. "This isn't something to be taken lightly, and it's certainly not something to joke about!"

At that moment, Rae couldn't bring herself to care less. It didn't much matter to her what the Privy Council did or didn't do. They had tried to arrest her. Twice. She and the PC were no longer associated. If Carter still wasn't an integral part of the mix, she would have written them off completely. As it stood, she was content to make jokes from afar.

"Why not?" She tried to keep the sneer from her voice and remain respectful. "They tried to lock me up, Mom. They think I'm an abomination. Why on earth should I care what they do?"

"Because not all of them feel that way," Carter interrupted smoothly. He hadn't been amused by her sarcasm in the slightest, but he seemed to understand the basis for it. "In fact, after your little speech about Cromfield they're about as divided as I've ever seen them."

"Great," Rae muttered, "because that's exactly how we want the Privy Council. Erratic and unstable."

"Rather than united against you?" Carter raised his eyebrows. "Yes."

Another sarcastic reply rose to the tip of Rae's tongue, but her temper cooled as she studied the travelled and weary face of the man in front of her. "United against *us*," she corrected softly. For the first time since Carter arrived she gave him the hint of a smile. "I didn't know you were going to back me up about Cromfield. When I went in there that night...I was planning on doing it alone."

Carter stared at her for a brief moment before glancing quickly at the stove. "Yes, well, I think it's high time you no longer have to do things alone. You and your friends have been left to carry the weight of this by yourselves for quite long enough. It's time the rest of us took a stand."

"But, James," Beth put a gentle hand on his arm, "grateful as I am for your support of Rae back at Guilder, and I am *grateful*...what does that mean for you? Two acting presidents? How's that even possible? Who's the second president?"

Carter's shoulders sank and he looked abruptly tired. "Victor Mallins."

"*Victor Mallins*?!" Beth cried, smacking her hand on the counter. "He's insane!"

"Wait..." Rae said, trying to catch up. "Victor? He was that really old guy, right? The one who looks like the Ghost of Christmas Past?"

Beth leaned back against the wall with her arms folded tightly across her chest. "Victor Mallins is the oldest living member of the Council. He's been with it for the last three iterations, and, as such, he has some pretty, well, outdated ideas of how things should be run."

"Outdated," Carter laughed sarcastically, "that's putting it lightly."

"Let me rephrase," Beth's eyes narrowed, "radically conservative, extremist, asininely idiotic ideas about the way things should be run."

"He was the strongest voice of opposition to opening the doors of Guilder to women," Carter continued, casting Rae a sideways glance.

"He's basically the sole reason I was never allowed to go," Beth fumed. From the look on her face, Rae gathered that the exclusion was a slight that would never fade, no matter how many years had passed. "As a result, every woman in my generation gifted with ink, not to mention the countless generations of woman before them, have no formal tatù education whatsoever. If some of us didn't happen to be gifted with powers that could be used in the service of the Council, we would never have had any training... period." She tossed back her hair, seemingly oblivious to the fact that both her hands had started smoking. "And as I recall, Mallins did everything in his power to stop *that* integration from happening as well."

Carter lowered his voice as his face grew grave. "More importantly, he was the man who led the witch-hunt for your father, back in the day. He fiercely hated all hybrids and everything your father stood for. And as such..."

Rae sighed as his meaning suddenly clicked. "...and as such, he despises me."

Carter's eyes locked on her and he finally nodded. "Despises *and* fears. The latter he would never admit. It's impossible to say which he feels more. But whatever the case, Victor Mallins is not a man you want working against you."

Rae pushed back from the table, temper rising in spite of her efforts to keep calm. "Well, it looks like the cat's out of the bag on that one. He already knows that I'm a hybrid, and he's already the co-president of the Privy Council. So why on earth does it matter to me now?"

"It matters," Carter interjected, "because he wants to offer you a job."

Rae's eyebrows shot to the ceiling as her jaw fell to the table. "Wait... What did you just say? Did I miss a step somewhere?"

There was a quick knocking on the already-opened door, and Julian, Molly, and Devon made their way cautiously into the kitchen. They had made themselves scarce as well, following Gabriel and Kraigan out to the barn. Seeing that no Privy Council guards had showed up yet to arrest them all, they had all apparently decided it was safe to come inside.

"Good to see you, sir." Devon crossed the kitchen quickly and shook Carter's hand.

Carter smiled warmly and clapped him on the back, doing the same with Julian when he arrived.

Rae took in each detail with a thoughtful frown.

Shaking hands? Sir?

The boys remembered they had quit the Privy Council, didn't they?

"I'm sorry I didn't see you coming," Julian was saying when she tuned back in. "We've been dealing with other things. I would've told Beth so she could prepare—"

"Nonsense," Carter answered quickly, "it was a spur of the moment decision. I wasn't sure when I'd be able to take my leave. Things have been rather up in the air since you left."

At the same time, both boys flushed with matching guilty expressions.

As quickly as they'd come, Carter instantly dismissed them. "I don't blame you in the slightest for walking away," he said seriously, looking at each one in turn. "Cromfield had just been exposed. The Council was in an uproar. To be honest, it was probably the best thing you could have done at that moment."

At that moment.

Rae's eyes narrowed. She sensed a sales pitch coming on...

"But for better or worse, the pieces on the board have begun to settle and it's time to get a few things back in order."

Devon looked at his old boss with a confused frown. "A few things back in order?"

Carter flashed him another fond smile. "Meaning *you*. All of you. I've been sent by the Council as a show of good faith. They want to offer all of you your old jobs back. You can be agents again. All you have to do is say yes, and return with me to London for a proper debrief."

His remark was met by a profound silence.

Molly looked wary, Julian simply looked surprised, and Devon looked...*excited*?

"Well, that's great!" he exclaimed, taking an automatic step closer to Carter. "I mean, as long as Rae's name is completely cleared—"

"And it is," Carter assured them all quickly. Both Devon and Beth sighed in relief. "I made her case personally, argued it in front of the Council when you left. They put it to an official vote. Not only will there be no further charges brought against Miss Kerrigan, but she and the rest of you are to be officially invited back and compensated for any time lost while under investigation."

Devon was practically beaming at the news.

Rae was not as convinced. "How close was the vote?" she muttered, spinning her coffee mug nervously on the table.

Julian looked just as hesitant as Rae. "What're they planning to do about Cromfield? Are they recognizing him as an official threat?"

"They're opening up an official investigation," Carter replied. "Once they finish raiding the catacombs beneath St. Stephen's Church, I suspect it won't be long before he's formally listed as an enemy of the state. At that point, I suspect we'll have to brief the royals, and teams will be launched in the hopes of finding him."

"Well they're not going to find him," Rae blurted, feeling something akin to whiplash at this sudden turn of events. "He wrote me a letter right before we left London. Sent it back with what was left of Gabriel. He's going *underground*, whatever that means."

Rae hadn't realized she'd done anything wrong. She didn't think she'd said a single thing out of line until Molly elbowed her sharply between the shoulder blades. At the same time, Carter suddenly frowned.

"Cromfield gave a letter to *Gabriel*? To *what was left* of Gabriel? What on earth are you talking about? Is Gabriel alright?"

Stupid! Stupid! Stupid!

Rae's heart froze in her chest. If only she had a tatù that allowed her to go back in time. On the other hand, Carter was sure to find out sooner or later. Maybe it was best he found out when Gabriel wasn't actually here to feel his wrath.

"Well...um..." she stammered, trying to find the words to make the whole terrible thing as palatable as possible. "The thing about Gabriel is that he is—I mean, he *was*—and that part's very important to understand, he *was*..."

"Gabriel was a spy for Cromfield," Beth finished calmly, looking Carter straight in the eyes.

Carter turned a dangerous shade of white. "No. Gabriel is no spy. I vetted him myself—"

"And he confessed it and apologized to me personally," Beth finished.

Rae looked at her in surprise. *He did? When?*

Carter was in a similar state of shock. "No, I just...I can't believe that." He started pacing without seeming to realize it. "I trusted him. With everything that was most important. He couldn't just... And now it turns out he's another..." The pacing stopped abruptly as his face hardened in cold fury. "Where is he? Still in London? When I get my hands on—"

"He's actually in the barn," Beth answered steadily. "He fled upon your arrival. And James, you're not going to lay a single hand on him."

Carter looked like she'd punched him in the face. "But Beth—"

"But nothing. To begin with, Cromfield beat you to the punch. *Literally*. The poor boy was half dead when he showed up here. He saved Rae's life. He didn't have to. He had the opportunity to turn her over to Cromfield, as well as the pieces of Simon's device, and he chose to remain with us instead. To help us work against him. That's worth something. We're in no position to be turning away allies, especially now."

Carter opened his mouth to argue, but Rae's mother's eyes narrowed in warning.

"*Especially* a child who was brainwashed and raised not to know any better," she continued. "We're not spilling any more blood because of Jonathon Cromfield. Not after..."

Her face suddenly fell and Carter looked up in concern.

"Not after what, Beth?"

Beth tried to answer, but for the first time in all Rae's memory she was at a loss. Rae got up instead and crossed the kitchen to take her mother's hand. If she couldn't say it, Rae would say it for her. There was no need for her to relive it yet again.

She looked straight into Carter's eyes and took a deep breath.

"Jennifer Jones is dead."

Those four words stopped the impromptu meeting right in its tracks. For the rest of the day, Carter and Beth went off together, walking along the fields. Rae suspected that her mother was finally having a good cry, a good scream, and whatever else she needed to do to reconcile the betrayal and subsequent death of her best friend.

But back at the house things were just getting started.

"Okay, okay, what is it?" Devon asked with a grin as Rae shoved him into their bedroom upstairs. "What is so important that you had to—"

"'*Well that's great*'?" Rae quoted in an accusing hiss. "*Well that's great* that we can go back to our jobs at the Privy Council like nothing ever happened?"

Devon froze in his tracks, the smile slipping off his face as he stared back at her. "That's what this is about? You're angry that—"

"Why the hell wouldn't I be angry, Devon? We left for a reason, you know."

He raised his hands peacefully, trying to stop the momentum of the conversation. "Yeah, we left because there was a chance they could still arrest you, and we left because they weren't going to do anything about Cromfield. Now both things are changed. They've formally apologized for how they've treated you—and you heard Carter—Cromfield's going to be Public Enemy Number One."

She didn't relax her posture, and he leaned in coaxingly.

"So...what's the problem?"

Her blue eyes narrowed. "The problem is they *did* arrest me, Devon. The problem is that no matter how hard Carter tries to smooth things over, most of the men on that Council still absolutely hate me and everything I represent. And that's never going to change! How could I work for them?"

"Come on," he tried to take her hand, "you don't know that. You could be the one who opens their eyes. Just like you were the one who got them to open the doors to Guilder—"

"I didn't ask Guilder to open its doors to me, or any other female!" She pulled away. "You can be so naïve! Of *course* they're never going to come around. The new guy who's in charge with Carter—this Victor—he's as old-school as they come! Probably older than Guilder!"

"I'm not being naïve, I'm being practical. All those things you were fighting against, they're all starting to change—one by one. You're the one who said you wanted to get rid of Cromfield so that you and I could have any chance at a normal life. How do you think we're going to do that on our own? It would be next to impossible. But with the resources of the Council behind us—"

"Oh, your precious freakin' Council!" Rae threw up her hands in exasperation. "You've always had such a one-track mind when it comes to them. It's like you're wearing blinders!"

"Now hold on a second." It was his turn to get angry, "I'm the one who turned my life upside down by turning my back on the Council to side with *you*. I'm the one who got kicked out of my home, my job—and for most of the summer even my country, because I was following *you*. Not them. *You*. So don't tell me that I'm blind when it comes to the Council. If anything, I'm blind when it comes to you."

Rae's heart was pounding and she was breathing in quick, shallow gasps. Nothing he was saying was untrue. She knew that. Every point he'd just made was dead right. Except...things couldn't just go back to the way they used to be. Too much had happened. Too much had changed. They were forgetting one very important thing.

"What about the hybrids?" she asked softly. "Camille, and Matti, and all of the rest of them—on the run because the people you're so quick to swear your allegiance to won't allow them to exist?"

For the first time, Devon paused. His eyes softened, and this time when he reached for her she allowed him to take her hand. "I know how you feel about the hybrids. I feel the same way, but I know you also feel...responsible for them. Rae, the best way to give them the best chance they can have is by working from the inside. You know that. Why are you fighting this?"

"Because we can't just go back!" she cried, pulling away from him once again. "Things aren't the same, Devon. We're...we're not the same!"

He stopped dead in his tracks, barely breathing as he looked at her. "We're not the same, as in...the four of us? Or..." his voice became very quiet, "or you and I aren't the same?"

His question caught Rae like a punch to the gut. She had been talking about the four of them, their quest to find Cromfield. But hearing it said aloud, she wondered if she hadn't meant the latter as well, without realizing it herself.

The silence stretched on as she struggled to find the right words. The longer it lasted, the paler Devon became. Finally, he turned abruptly on his heel. "I'll leave you alone so you can figure it out."

Rae's eyes filled up with tears as she watched him go. "Devon, wait—"

But much to her surprise he didn't leave. He held open the door her for her to do so. When she simply stared in confusion, his lips turned up into a hard smile—the smile he saved for people he didn't care for, never the smile he used with her. "I'm guessing you'll probably want to talk to...some people. To help you work it out."

Gabriel.

He didn't say the name, yet it rang out loud and clear between them.

"Devon," she said quietly as she crossed over to the door, "this has nothing to do with him. This is you and me, and the kind of future we want. It's about whether or not that future involves the Privy Council." She said the words confidently, although a small stubborn part of her still wasn't so sure.

He didn't move his position in the slightest, but stared down at her intently. "Good. I really hope that's true. But either way I want you to be sure. I wasn't kidding, Rae. I've turned my life inside out to make this happen. If there are parts to it you're rethinking...well, I want you to be perfectly clear. I think we owe each other that."

She fought back the tears and nodded quietly. He was right again. He was always right.

Before they could move forward they had to figure out where they were moving to. The offer from the Privy Council complicated things for her. She didn't know what working for them would imply. He was clear on this. She wasn't. And Gabriel...?

She needed time.

"Okay," she said shakily, "I guess I'll just...um...I'll see you at dinner."

"Sure," he flashed a softer smile then shut the door behind her, leaving her alone in the hall. At least she thought she was alone.

"Watch it," Kraigan complained as she turned and bumped him hard in the shoulder. "Some of us are still recovering from your electricity-happy friend."

"Yeah," she mumbled, hardly hearing what he was saying, "sorry." She felt like a strong wind had come and literally sucked the life out of her. There was a strange tingling all over her body, and it felt as though she was floating down the stairs.

How had things gotten so out of hand so quickly? One minute she and Devon were discussing potential job offers, and the next second it spiked into their entire future? And then how the hell had Gabriel gotten into the mix? Devon was so sure that he was what she was talking about, but she hadn't put two and two together herself.

Was he right again? Did Gabriel play a bigger part in all of this than she was giving him credit for?

A wave of nausea overtook her and she half crumbled against the banister on the stairs.

No. She wasn't going to walk away. She didn't need space. She may not know *what* she wanted, but she knew *who* she wanted.

And that was the person she needed to talk with if she was indeed going to be planning out her future. It wasn't a one-way decision. She and Devon were in a committed relationship. That made it a discussion. And one that she planned on having right now.

On a wave of adrenaline, she turned and doubled back up the stairs, practically flying as she rushed back down the hall to their shared room. She was just gearing up for exactly what she was going to say, but the second she touched the handle she heard a soft *thud* on the other side.

"Dev?" she asked with a frown, leaning closer to hear.

There was no response, nothing but the soft swishing of the wind through the open bedroom window. An instinct she didn't understand made her freeze in place.

She hadn't left the window open.

"Devon?" she cried again, pushing open the door.

There he was, twitching uncontrollably in the middle of the floor. His eyes were dilated and disoriented—a specific look she'd seen on several occasions now before. Occasions that always seemed to involve one person in particular.

Her eyes drifted up to the open window, the curtains swaying in the breeze.

Kraigan.

Chapter 8

"HELP! SOMEBODY HELP! PLEASE!!" Rae shrieked before turning back to Devon, who was still lying on the floor. "It's okay, honey, it's going to be okay. HELP, DAMN IT! Just sit up, baby. It's alright."

Julian and Molly appeared in the doorway the next second, breathless from having bolted up the stairs when they heard her scream. Gabriel was just a second after them.

"What the hell happened?!" Julian demanded, sinking to his knees beside his friend. "Dev, what the...?" He pulled him into a delicate sitting position and leaned him back against the bed. "How did I not see it? Who did this?"

"It's Kraigan," Rae growled, her eyes flicking again to the open window.

Of course it was Kraigan. She should have known it the second he bumped into her in the hall. She should have recognized the feeling of having one of her tatùs taken away. She had been so caught up in the fight with Devon, she'd attributed *that* to the strange, hollow feeling that swept over her. The wave of nausea and the internal crumble that followed.

All things that she was seeing on Devon's face right now.

"I'm sorry, Rae," he was mumbling, trying to control his trembling hands. "I'm so sorry."

"Sorry!" She knelt directly in front of him, taking his face in her hands. "Devon, you've *nothing* to be sorry for! I'm the idiot who let him stay in this house."

The front door slammed hard beneath them, and they all suddenly realized Molly was gone.

"She's not going to catch him," Devon muttered, holding on to the base of the bed like his life depended on it. "He took my tatù."

Julian's eyes flashed momentarily white before returning with pity to his friend. "No, she's not going to catch him."

Of the four of them, Gabriel was the only one still frozen in place, staring out the open window like he couldn't wrap his head around what was happening.

"Kraigan?" he repeated softly, eyes on the horizon. "I just can't believe... I mean, I thought he was starting to—"

"Yes, of course it was Kraigan!" Rae snapped. As conflicted as she might have felt a moment or two before, it was suddenly incredibly easy for her to prioritize the men in her life. Devon had warned against Kraigan at every step. Gabriel had welcomed him with open arms just to get farther into her good graces. "Of course it was Kraigan, because that's exactly what Kraigan does!" She shot him a fierce glare before turning back to Devon. "I should have seen this coming," she said again, stroking back his hair as he struggled to regain his senses.

There was nothing more disorienting than having a tatù stripped away. It flipped your entire world up on its head. And if that was the only tatù you had? Rae couldn't even imagine...

"It's not your fault," Devon repeated, pulling himself up as he took several steadying deep breaths. "I let him get too close. Actually reached out to shake his hand when he offered..."

Julian's expression darkened to something that gave Rae actual chills, but she kept her attention on the problem at hand, replaying Devon's words with a frown. "Why would he want to shake your hand first? He didn't need to do that to touch you..."

In fact, Kraigan didn't need to take Devon's tatù at all. He was still walking around with Jennifer's stolen leopard. A tatù that, even as Rae thought about it, she felt float to the surface right back where it belonged. That only begged the question: Why take Devon's? To be frank, while they were both powerful

Jennifer's was more Kraigan's style. It was brutal, raw strength—
an animalistic powerhouse that had no real match. Devon's,
while absurdly strong in its own right, implied a bit more finesse.
Something that Kraigan valued about as highly as things like
serving spoons and basic human decency. There was just no place
for it in his life.

That meant he wasn't replacing the leopard with the fox; he
was simply stealing another offensive tatù. Something fast to help
him get away because the ink he'd stolen from Rae was lacking in
both departments. This, of course, led to the obvious question.

Which of Rae's tatùs did he take? She couldn't remember
what one she'd used last.

As if Devon had heard her whole internal diatribe out loud,
he slowly lifted his eyes to see her. "Rae, he didn't just take my
tatù." He swallowed hard. "He used Carter's on me. That's why
he grabbed my hand."

It was as if someone had poured a stream of cold water down
Rae's spine. All the color drained from her face as she slowly
pieced together the implications of what that meant.

Kraigan knew about the hybrids. He knew about Angel and
Gabriel and everything they and Jennifer had stood for. He knew
every inch of the Guilder underground as it had been memorized
in Devon's mind. But even worse...

Kraigan knew about Cromfield.

And now he was gone.

Ignoring Julian's words of caution, Devon pulled himself to
his feet, leaning heavily on the bed as he tried to find his balance.
"I wish that was all," he panted with the strain as his eyes flicked
once again to Rae's before landing on the open window. "Rae...he
took the serum."

"How could you be so stupid!"

It wasn't Devon who took the censure, or even Gabriel. It was Rae.

She was expecting it. To be frank, a part of her almost welcomed it and she bowed her head under Carter's ranting without putting up the slightest bit of resistance. At least someone was seeing things clearly. She needed a strong dose of reality to help open her eyes.

"He helped us take down Jennifer," she said softly. It wasn't an excuse, merely an explanation. "And I didn't think I could keep sleeping with one eye open for the rest of my life. I figured some kind of truce had to be made."

Gabriel stepped bravely in between them, still sporting a painful limp. "It isn't her fault, sir. I was the one who tried to include Kraigan, tried to make him...fit in around here."

Carter's eyes flashed dangerously and he fell instantly silent. "As for you, Mr. Alden, I think you would do best to hold your tongue and keep a low profile whilst I'm in this house. The Kerrigans and their friends may have found it in themselves to forgive you for your betrayal, but rest assured, Gabriel—*I'm not there yet.*"

Gabriel gulped and fell back in line. "Of course, I'm...I'm sorry. Sir."

Carter rolled his eyes and continued to chastise Rae for her carelessness, a well-earned rant she half-absorbed and half-tuned out while studying a crack in the tile beneath her feet.

The rest of the kitchen was in a similar state of unrest.

Julian sat perched in the corner, his eyes flashing in and out of time as he searched for any sign of Kraigan. Molly still hadn't returned from her personal quest to catch him, while Devon, aiming slightly lower, was trying to make himself a cup of coffee without any degree of success.

Without a sense of balance or even basic depth perception, he kept either over-shooting everything or flat out spilling every time his fingers would sporadically spasm. The attempt left him with a small pool of espresso on the counter and an empty cup.

Eventually, when his efforts became too pathetic to ignore, Carter turned around with a hint of frustration. "Mr. Wardell, either let me do that for you or have Miss Kerrigan conjure you one."

Devon blushed and gave up on the whole enterprise altogether, tripping his way awkwardly to the table and pulling out a chair. Rae followed his movements sympathetically whilst vaguely noting that she was back to 'Miss Kerrigan.' She'd really messed up big this time.

But before she could conjure a thing for Devon the front door flew open and Molly stormed inside, little bits of dirt and grass clinging to her purple leggings.

"Kraigan's gone," she gasped, still out of breath from the run. "I managed to hit him with a single blast but it hardly even slowed him down. That tatù of Devon's is a nightmare to chase!"

"Glad someone's enjoying it," Devon mumbled pitifully, still twirling his empty mug between his fingers. It slipped at the last second and fell to the floor with an incriminating *crash*.

The girls just stared at it. Carter and Julian stared at it. Not one of them could remember the last time they'd seen Devon do anything even remotely clumsy. It simply wasn't in his nature.

But as quickly as the mug had fallen, Gabriel replaced it with another one already full of steaming cappuccino. He alone seemed to think this Kraigan mess was entirely his fault, and he slid the new mug apologetically between Devon's fingers, casting him a nervous glance as he did. "No big deal," he said lightly, a little too lightly to pass as casual. "I'll clean this up."

Instead of taking the coffee Devon stood abruptly from the table and walked outside, Julian and Molly right on his heels. He may not blame Gabriel for Kraigan, but he blamed him for a whole host of other problems and he was in no mood to make him feel better about any of them today.

"Just let them go," Rae said softly as Gabriel made to follow. She watched through the window as the two guys headed across the property to the open field just beyond. "You've no idea how it feels to lose your ink. He needs some space."

Gabriel's face tensed and he stared down at the table, a thousand thoughts warring behind his green eyes. "Rae, I'm really, *really* sorry about Kraigan—"

"You need to let that go too," Rae interrupted, turning to him for the first time. "Carter's right. This is my fault. You didn't know what Kraigan was. I did. I have no idea what I was thinking letting him stay here."

"You were thinking he's your brother," Gabriel said softly.

It was Carter who answered him. "Kraigan doesn't know how to be family to anyone. He's been warped beyond repair. All that remains now is a monster."

"People can change," Gabriel countered just as softly, refusing to meet Carter's eyes. "If you give them a chance, they can surprise you." The words were bold though he spoke cautiously—respectfully, even.

Either way, Carter wasn't having it. "Mr. Alden, if you wouldn't mind stepping outside, or upstairs, or really anywhere that gets you out of my sight, Miss Kerrigan and I have some things we need to discuss."

Gabriel's face tightened for a split second before he cleared it with that same deliberate nonchalance. "Of course," he murmured. Then to Rae, "I'll be right upstairs if anyone needs me."

Their eyes met briefly and she sensed a great deal more beneath the words, but she lowered her eyes quickly to the table. Like she said—she was in enough trouble already.

"No one will," Carter answered, dismissing him with a rude wave. When he was gone, Carter turned back to Rae with a hint of frustration. "Miss Kerrigan, I'm not going to lie. When I went out on a limb and staked my entire career and reputation for you, claimed that you had nothing but the Privy Council's best interests at heart, I had every confidence that what I was saying was true."

Rae blanched. "And now?"

"Now I'm wondering why, when I brought you an official pardon and offered you your job back, you looked at me like I'd shot your dog."

Rae sighed. She wasn't ready to have this conversation so soon after already trying and failing to have it with Devon. The Council had burned her, and continued to blatantly scorn the rest of her hybrid counterparts. Wasn't that enough reason to grant her time to think? Why was everyone rushing this?

The clock ticked loudly on the wall behind them, highlighting her problem in an ironically literal way. But when she finally looked up and met Carter's eyes there was no defiance, just the cold, hard facts. "Have you ever heard of a family called the Padrons?" she asked quietly.

"The Padrons?" Carter repeated, a little shaken by the change of subject. "No, why?"

"You should have," Rae continued in the same soft monotone. "Their young boy, Matti, should be gearing up to go to Guilder in just a few years. But he can't. Because he's in hiding." She leaned back in her chair, looking decidedly grim. "Because he's a hybrid."

Carter paused, and she used the moment to press her advantage.

"Do I have to add 'like me,' or do you get where I'm going with this?"

There was a sudden creak as Carter pulled out the chair across from her and settled himself down with a glare. "You know, I've long pushed for Guilder to add a class on basic etiquette to their current curriculum. If there was a way to erase poorly-timed sarcasm from teenagers, I'd move heaven and earth to do it."

Rae leaned forward with a glare of her own. "I'm sorry if I'm trying to temper my frustrations with humor rather than with something more volatile. But the fact remains. How can you expect me to go back and work for the same people who are actively perpetuating that kind of discrimination against the very people I've been battling to positively represent? What kind of hypocrite would that make me?"

Carter took off his jacket and rubbed his eyes, looking just as abruptly exhausted as he had when he'd first arrived. "Rae, no one understands the need for hybrid equality more than me, but I'm telling you that you cannot throw away your entire future in response to a problem that's plagued our kind of people from the beginning of time. You need to work within the system—"

She snorted. "You sound like Devon."

Carter looked up sharply. "Devon Wardell is an exceptionally bright young man. One who's given up a lot to help get you where you are today. You'd do well to listen to him."

Rae's eyes flashed as she folded her arms across her chest. "Lanford said almost those same words to me the first year I was here. He turned out to be traitor." She glared at Carter. "Tell me something: If the Privy Council had known about Cromfield and the list from the beginning—if they were the ones who had sent the four of us to track them all down—why would they be doing it?"

"What do you mean?"

"They'd send us out after the hybrids just to keep them from Cromfield, so that he wouldn't get any stronger. It would've had nothing to do with saving their lives, because in the eyes of the Council, they shouldn't even exist. *I* shouldn't even exist." Her blood raced hot through her veins as she tried to keep her voice steady. "And now you're telling me that I should be grateful that they think I'm useful enough to keep around? I should be grateful that they haven't labeled me 'potentially dangerous' enough to throw me in one of their dungeons? That I should be *so grateful* that I'll put on their little leash and come back and work for them? That's what you're saying?"

Silence fell between them as both retreated to their chairs. The little room filled up with the sound of quick, agitated breathing.

When Carter spoke, he was quiet and calm. Eerily calm. "You think you're the only one with a stake in this?" he murmured, barely loud enough for her to hear.

She switched into Devon's tatù with a frown, making sure she'd understood. "Excuse me?"

Carter sat back abruptly, looking at Rae with speculative restraint. "I'm in love with your mother. You know this?"

Rae's mouth fell wide open. Her mind scrambled as she tried to figure out where he was going with that, but it kept circling back to a single, terrifying thought. She'd known. Just refused to admit it to herself.

Carter as a stepfather.

"I...uh..." She blushed and tucked her hair back behind her ears. "I try not to think about it, to be honest..."

"Well, I am," Carter said firmly. While his voice was calm his eyes were a whirlwind of emotions, each one battling for supremacy over the next. "And if she would ever do me the honor of letting me share in her life...I've to come to terms with a simple thing." His voice dropped to something scarcely above a whisper. "She and I could never have children."

For the second time that day Rae felt like something punched her in the gut. Her eyes welled up with tears before she could stop them, and she lowered her head quickly to the table so Carter wouldn't see her cry. "Because...they might be like me?" she asked in a broken voice just as soft as his.

"No, Rae!" The next second Carter was on her side of the table, sinking down in the chair beside her and taking her hand. "If Beth and I were blessed to have a child as spirited and intelligent, as gifted and brave...well, I couldn't ask for anything more."

Still on the verge of tears Rae finally lifted her eyes to see him. She didn't think they'd ever been so close before, not even when he was using his ability to stare inside her head. She could see every single flick of hazel in his eyes. Every single line of worry etched into his forehead.

As she stared something he'd said earlier suddenly made sense. He'd been ranting about the sting of Gabriel's betrayal, because Gabriel had been entrusted with the most important things.

She just now realized that in Carter's mind, one of those things was her.

"But I see what this world has *done* to you," he continued. "I see the horrors and dangers it's put you through. I see the walls you've had to put up; I know how hard it is for you to trust. And no matter how hard your mother, Mr. Wardell, or I constantly try to stop it, it seems as though there's always someone new on the horizon waiting to do you harm." He pulled back and shook his head, completely unaware that Beth was standing in the doorway behind them, silent as a ghost. "No, I could not bring another hybrid child into a world such as this," he said again. However, despite the deep sadness written on his face, his eyes flashed up with determination. "That's why people like you and I have to do everything in our power to change it."

A bit overwhelmed, Rae leaned back and dropped her eyes to the table, thinking hard as she bit her lip with a little frown. She had never thought of it that way. She had always considered hybrids in terms of retribution for those already scorned, not paving the way for those yet to come.

And what of children she and Devon would have? Sure, it wasn't something they'd ever talked about but that's what *someday* was for, right? What if their children didn't get a someday because Rae was too entrenched in all the politics happening right now to lift her eyes to the future?

Beth peeled herself away from the wall and settled down on the other side of Carter, silently taking his hand as they both watched Rae, giving her time to think.

When she was finally finished she stared up at the both of them—two of the people most harmed, and yet, made strongest by this whole ordeal, the decision already simmering around in her head strengthened with resolve. "And you really think we can best accomplish that by working with the Privy Council?"

There were no more word games between her and Carter now. No more sarcastic jibes or displays of power. Just the plain truth. And the road to get there.

"It's the single ruling body of government in our society," he said simply. "If there's ever to be any kind of social change, it'll start there. Someone just needs to be there to start it."

Rae shook her head helplessly. "And you think that someone should be me?"

All at once both Carter and Beth's faces relaxed into twin smiles. They shared a knowing look before turning those smiles to Rae.

"No, honey," Beth said warmly, taking her hand, "we *know* it should be you."

Rae hesitated, thinking of the path they were considering and mentally bracing herself against everything that was sure to follow. "I make a lot of mistakes," she said nervously, thinking back on everything from getting outmatched by Cromfield to this newest mishap with Kraigan.

Carter smiled. "That's why you need a strong group of people around you to help."

Rae's eyes drifted to the window where her friends were having a silent argument. As if on cue, Devon slipped where he was standing and the other two lowered their heads slowly to peer at him on the ground. "...Great."

Beth grinned. "You'll figure it out. Lord knows we did." She gestured to herself and Carter.

"What does that mean?"

Carter squeezed Beth's hand. "One of us becomes the President of the Privy Council while the other rises up to become one of the greatest agents the Privy Council has ever known—a woman takes that prize? Yes, Rae, we are firm believers in changing things from within the system."

The corners of Rae's lips turned up in a sly little grin. "Hate to break it to you, Carter, but you're only one of two sitting presidents on the Privy Council."

Carter accepted that wisdom with a wry smile of his own. "That's true. Just one of the many things we'll be attempting to set right."

"First on the list."

The words were out of Rae's mouth before she realized she'd said them, and both Carter and Beth shared a quick glance before looking back at her with hopeful smiles.

"What exactly does that mean?" Beth asked, unable to keep a note of pride from her voice.

Rae sighed, glancing out the window at her friends as the chapter before them was suddenly made clear. "That means...we're going back to London."

Chapter 9

There was a special moment hidden inside every London morning, a moment when the whole world seemed to stop. A mere split second in time—the moment just before sunrise. As if the city itself was taking a breath before starting the day.

Blink and you'd miss it.

Rae never blinked. Over the last couple of years she'd come to understand that she couldn't really count on anything. People, places, idealisms, beliefs. Plans for the future, visions of the past. They could be rock-solid one moment, and then the next—gone; almost as if they'd never existed in the first place.

But she could count on this moment. This solitary instant of peace and quiet. A suspended flicker in time where she could gather her thoughts, close her eyes, and simply breathe.

CRASH!

The sound of shattering glass brought her back to earth.

"Sorry!" Devon called as she whirled around in panic, slopping a good deal of her morning coffee down the front of her robe. "Sorry again," he muttered, staring down guiltily at the box of broken cocktail glasses she and Molly had purchased for the apartment.

Rae's eyes swept over the crystal shards and she fought back a sigh. This wasn't the first one of these accidents they'd had even this morning. It most likely wouldn't be the last.

"It's okay," she reassured him, kneeling down to help clean up the mess. The front of her silken robe was hot-glued to her chest with spilled cappuccino, but she maintained a careful smile.

Devon was not so careful, his utter frustration clearly written all over his face. "I got it," he muttered sullenly, pushing away her hands. In the process he accidently cut himself on a piece of glass, adding a bright sprinkling of blood to the shattered pieces. "*Damn it*!" He pulled back with a hiss, holding up his sliced fingers. "Are you *kidding* me?!"

Rae bowed her head and bit down on her lip. As someone who had lived in the constant shadow of Devon's almost superman-esque dependability these last few years, the loss of his tatù and the overwhelming discoordination that followed it could be seen as just a *little bit* funny. She knew she wasn't the only one who thought so. Although, she was the only one who had the sensitivity and tact to keep it to herself.

Regardless, she hoped that wherever he was, Kraigan would just pick up a new ability already so that Devon could get his back. It was as though someone had clipped his wings. And try as he might to take it one day at a time, she didn't know how much more his frayed nerves could take.

"I mean, *really*?!" He cursed again, throwing down the pieces he was holding in disgust. "Is this how you guys feel all the time? This weak and pathetic?"

He misinterpreted the look on Rae's face and clarified.

"I mean, not *you*. *You* still have my ability." He scowled and made no effort whatsoever to keep the resentment off his face. "But the rest of the world, Molly, Julian?" He shook some droplets of blood from his fingers to emphasize his point. "Is this *normal*?!"

"Hey," Rae wrapped his hand in a dishtowel before kissing him gently on the wrist, "I think you've just learned to rely a little too much on your tatù to do things for you. It'll come back."

"What?" he sulked, staring at his hand like it had offended him. "My ink or my innate ability to walk without falling down like the rest of you cavemen?"

Rae's lips twitched, but she held it together. "Your ink. Kraigan's a jealous little demon. He can't be around people with tatùs for very long before needing to steal someone else's. You'll get yours back; you just need to hang in there until you do."

When he continued to pout, she kissed further and further up his arm, ending with his lips and coaxing out a reluctant smile with one of her own.

"In the meantime maybe you should refrain from carrying boxes of glass. And, like...using the blender and stuff."

He stared into her eyes, looking absolutely heartbroken. "How will I make my smoothies?"

She snorted with laughter. "You don't drink smoothies."

"I could start to. I think I could learn to like them." He gazed mournfully at the broken glasses. "Now I'll never get the chance."

"Tell you what," she giggled again and kissed him again, "I'll make your smoothies."

He held his hurt hand up in the air while the other snaked around her back, tugging her teasingly into his lap. She straddled him with a grin, brushing his dark hair out of his eyes. Despite all recent evidence to the contrary, and though he'd never admit it to himself, Devon didn't particularly need his tatù. He was already strong and fast and a naturally gifted fighter. That being said, she rarely, if ever, got to see this side of him. All his moping aside, it was kind of adorable. For possibly the first time since they'd met *he* needed someone to take care of *him*.

With a mischievous grin Rae pulled sharply on his hair, snapping his head back so it was tilted up towards hers.

"Miss Kerrigan, it would be most unfair to take advantage of me in this state," he teased, eyes sparkling as he stared hungrily at her lips. "I'm clearly not at my best."

"Are you kidding?" Rae grinned. "It might be the only chance I ever get to control you. You could be my man-servant. I could send you out to do my bidding."

He chuckled and glanced once more at the broken glasses. "As long as it isn't anything too important we should be fine."

As if on cue, the door swung open and Molly and Julian breezed inside. While Julian was laden down with boxes, Molly was carrying nothing but her bedazzled cell phone and a miniature mug of espresso. Once they were inside she pointed to where Julian was to discard the boxes, and pulled off her oversized sunglasses with a look of dismay. "Another one bites the dust, huh?" Her eyes swept over the crystal in question before narrowing abruptly. "Oh *Devon*! The *Waterford*? Why were you even holding that?"

"It's not his fault," Julian said, his eyes twinkling, "he's like a toddler learning to walk for the first time."

Molly swung around with her hands on her hips. "That's kind of my point. You don't give a box full of high quality crystal stemware to a toddler!"

"It's not my fault!" Devon exclaimed, burying his face in his hands. "I had no idea what kind of lesser world the lot of you have been living in. It's demoralizing as hell. How do you guys even walk down the stairs?"

Molly smirked. "A lot better than you. I saw you fall earlier today."

Devon's high cheekbones went pink as he dropped his eyes to the floor. "I didn't think anyone was around."

"It's going to get better, man," Julian said comfortingly, clapping him on the back. "You only tripped once while getting ready today. And for a masochistic moment I almost even considered letting you drive. Then I thought of the pedestrians..."

"Oh shut up, Jules. You have no idea what it's like."

Julian raised his eyebrows. "I have no idea what it's like not to have super speed and agility?"

"You know what I mean; you're all used to having things be so terrible. I've come to expect something better."

This time Rae had to duck her head to hide her smile at the look on Julian's face. It was possible Devon didn't realize that in his quest for sympathy he was alienating a lot of people.

Julian shook his head in amused disbelief. "Welcome to reality, princess."

Devon ignored this and proceeded to try to pour himself some orange juice. The second before he did so, Julian's eyes flashed white and, though he remained quiet, his lips turned up in a secret, knowing smile. As Devon reached up to get the carton, his shoe caught on the edge of the counter and the whole thing slipped from his hands, exploding in the sink in a giant shower of orange spray.

As Devon blinked drops of juice from his desolate eyes, Rae shot Julian an accusatory glare, slipping into Maria's telepathy.

I saw that, jerk.

His eyes widened innocently as he mouthed *what?*

You know what.

He flashed an unapologetic grin, but went to help his friend clean up.

Meanwhile Rae tossed the last of the broken crystal into the bin and turned to Molly. "Don't worry. I'll conjure us some new stuff."

Molly shook her head with a sigh. "But it won't be Waterford."

"No, it'll be better," Rae tried to cheer her up. "It'll be magic!" She lifted her hands and was surprised when Molly slapped them back out of the air.

"We're not going for *magic* here, Rae! We're going for *normal*. Or at least as normal as things can get. No immortal villains, no mildewing hostels in Peru... just four friends who happen to have super powers, living it up in a London penthouse. Normal as that." She slapped Julian in the chest as his eyes went white again. "Did you not just hear me? Don't do that! With our luck you'll get some sort of vision that the world's about to end!"

"I'm just seeing what kind of parking there's going to be on Sixth."

Her face changed immediately. "Oh! Can you also check Keaston and Third?"

"I thought we were having a move-in day," Rae interjected, staring around the house full of unopened boxes. They'd made great progress while waiting for Gabriel to return, but they hadn't had much to unpack. Now that the bulk of their things had arrived from Guilder it felt a bit like they were back at square one.

"Can't," Molly said breezily, "I'm meeting Luke for breakfast."

Julian snatched an apple from the counter and headed for the door. "And some of us have our *own* place to move into," he added, casting Molly a bitter look. "You know, just in case anyone forgot and demanded help moving all *their* boxes instead."

"Jules, don't be absurd," she countered, tilting her head to the side as she examined her freshly painted nails. "You're not even halfway done unloading my storage box."

"Yeah," he laughed sarcastically, "that's what your boyfriend is for. I'm out. Later guys!"

"Wait—" Rae called, but he was already halfway to the landing.

"Yep!" Molly chirped. "See ya!"

"Molls—"

"I'm going to take a shower to rinse all this off," Devon murmured, still wringing streams of orange juice from his shirt.

Rae actually stamped her foot, unable to believe she'd been abandoned this easily. "Devon, you can't possibly be serious—"

"You're right," he added morosely, "I'll probably just drown."

Before she could stop him he vanished up the hall.

Three doors slammed in rapid succession, leaving Rae standing alone in the middle of the room, wondering where her quiet morning had gone...

After the second time Rae heard something fall in the shower, she decided to intervene. The door was closed but unlocked, and she crept silently forward, peering through the clouds of steam.

How was it that this was the boy she was dating?

For a second she just watched him from the doorway. It wasn't often she was able to catch him unawares, and she had to say she was thoroughly enjoying the unguarded view.

He looked like something out of a magazine, something that had been photo-shopped to perfection. His dark hair streamed down his neck as he ran his fingers through it in what looked like slow motion. It was only later Rae realized she was just used to seeing him move so fast. She could see every muscular outline in his arms and back, and for a moment, a brief, mischievous moment, she almost considered jumping right on top of him.

Then again, *today* he would probably drop her.

And then there was the other thing...

She folded her arms across her chest with a sigh. There was that pesky little other thing. She didn't know exactly where she and Devon stood. They were still together, of course, but they hadn't been able to patch things up since their argument back in Scotland.

Of course the fact that Rae decided to at least entertain the idea of giving London another chance made big strides towards reconciliation. And while her mother was distracted by the arrival of Carter, he was able to slip into her room that night with no one being the wiser.

But they hadn't talked. Or kissed. Or even held hands.

They simply slept together. By the time Rae opened her eyes the next morning he was already dressed and downstairs.

The kiss that had just happened in the kitchen, well, that had been a gamble. One that had most decidedly paid off. Being back in the city, with Guilder and the Council just an hour's drive away, it made it easy to forget everything that had happened in the interim. If the kitchen was any indication, Devon seemed to wholeheartedly agree. Gabriel was out of sight, staying at a hotel down the road, and although a part of her had never thought it would actually happen, Julian and Devon were actually moving in next door. Devon had a place but he and Julian opted for the apartment for now.

For the first time in a very, *very* long time, it felt like the beginning of something.

"*Shit*—Rae!" Devon whirled around with a gasp upon seeing her there. One hand flew up to his chest as the other shot out like a shield between them. He dropped them both with a sheepish look. "You scared me."

This time Rae couldn't help but laugh. It was all too strange. "You know, I've known you since I was fifteen, Devon, and I can honestly say I've never seen you jump like that."

"Shut up," he chuckled, reaching for the shampoo. "I didn't hear you come in... *Wait*," his face soured and he shot her an accusing glare, "I didn't hear you come in because you're using my tatù right now, aren't you?"

"Guilty." She grinned. "In my defense I did come in here with the good intention of conjuring you some hand rails..."

He shook his head disparagingly. "You have no shame."

All at once Rae froze. The words triggered a sudden echo in her, and despite all her good feelings about new beginnings she was suddenly taken back.

She had said those exact same words to Gabriel the morning she'd left to confront Jennifer. She'd been standing in clouds of steam then too—he was undressing to take a bath.

As if to bolster the memory, a familiar tangy scent caught her attention. She looked down to see bright orange swirls of juice still pouring off of Devon as he trailed his fingers through his wet hair. The sharp acidic smell brought to mind other memories as it circled its way down the drain. Memories of another naked man and the intoxicating smell of his body wash as it wafted over her.

Orange juice, she gritted her teeth. *Why did it have to be orange juice?*

The smell of citrus momentarily overwhelmed her, and she took a step back.

"I'm, um...I just going to..."

"Hey..." She looked up to see him staring at her curiously, a confused half-grin still lighting up his face as the water streamed down his body in tantalizing little rivulets. "I'm just kidding," he assured her quickly, misunderstanding her hesitation. The grin faded and he took a step out of the water to cup her cheek. "What's the matter? You look like you've seen a ghost..."

The warmth of his hand heated her skin, or maybe she was just blushing. Her heart stuttered and skipped as she stared up into his beautiful eyes. Thank heavens for once he couldn't hear it. "Nothing's the matter," she said in what she hoped was a steadier voice. "I was just going to conjure us some towels."

She took a step back and did exactly that, feeling oddly relieved that she was no longer channeling his ink. Just like that time on the boat when she'd fallen asleep in Gabriel's arms, it made her feel almost guilty to be using it. When she was finished, she reached up slowly and slipped off her sticky robe and then the shirt underneath. "How about it, Mr. Wardell?" she asked seductively. "Mind if I join you?"

He smiled again, stepping back under the torrents of hot water. "Miss Kerrigan, I thought you'd never ask..."

Much to Rae's delight their time in the shower went as well as their time in the kitchen. And created as much of a mess. There was a wet trail from when he'd suddenly turned off the water and carried her to her bed, and because she still had nothing to sleep on but a bare mattress both of them were sporting matching circular indentations in their skin from the springs.

"I look like a giraffe," she called, examining herself slowly in the mirror. The giant rings laced up her back like some kind of weird tattoo, offsetting the sparkling fairy on her lower back.

Devon appeared back in the doorway, holding a mug of coffee and a thermos. He was already dressed and dried and was gazing at her back with a look that sent flushes of heat careening down her skin. "You most definitely do not look like a giraffe," he promised, extending her the mug.

She took it gratefully then frowned at the thermos. "You're not staying?"

"I've got some work to do in the city," he explained, slipping on his shoes with one hand while balancing the thermos with the other. She watched nervously and prayed for the best. When he was finished he gave her a swift kiss on the forehead, followed by a wink. "You wanted a normal life, right? Well this is it. I'm a working man once again."

She folded her arms across her newly-conjured bathrobe with a pout—the coffee-stained one had already taken up residence in the trash. "What work do you have to do? We just got back..."

"Follow up on some old cases," he said casually, "get started on a written report. We missed a lot when we were gone this summer. There's a bunch to do."

Rae couldn't think of anything to say to this so she settled for a simple, "Oh."

She'd hoped that the four of them—or more specifically—the *two* of them would get at least a day to settle in before the Privy Council started taking over their lives. And considering none of them had technically accepted their positions yet, it was all still tentative, it hadn't seemed so unlikely. Maybe Devon was just being 'super-agent' like usual. After all, Molly and Julian weren't jumping back into the Council's chokehold. They were out having a day for themselves.

"Well, do you think you'll be back for dinner tonight?" she asked hopefully. "I can conjure us some," she backtracked quickly at the look on his face, "I mean, we can order some take-out."

"That sounds great." He gave her another kiss, on the lips this time, and pulled back with a smile. "This is going to be good, Rae. This is going to be what we wanted."

She forced herself to smile quickly in return, and waved goodbye as he headed out the door.

The tentative 'probationary return' had been her idea. This was their future they were talking about. There was bound to be a bit of trial and error before they got it right.

Julian and Molly had been quick to agree. Devon hesitated a bit more. She suspected that he was ready to jump right back into the saddle, but had gone along with it for their sakes. This morning, after seeing how excited he was to get out the door and back to work, a flutter of nerves swirled away in her stomach.

Were things really going to be good? Was this really what they wanted?

A knock on the door brought an automatic smile to her face. She pulled her new robe tighter around her and skipped across the kitchen floor to answer it.

"Did you fall down again, or did you want to break in that bed..."

Her voice trailed off when she saw who was on the other side.

"Miss Kerrigan," Victor said with a twisted smile, "I trust you're keeping busy?"

Chapter 10

"Aren't you going to invite me inside?"

Rae blinked. She realized she had been standing in the doorway, saying nothing for the better part of a minute. Perhaps it was the shock of seeing such a prominent member of the Privy Council darkening her doorstep. Perhaps she was simply hoping he'd go away. "Um, yes...I suppose."

She took a reluctant step back and watched as he walked inside, instantly wishing she was wearing anything other than a lilac bathrobe that stopped halfway down her thighs. But Victor Mallins couldn't have been less interested in her. His eyes swept over the decadent furniture, the vaulted ceilings, and the stacks of unopened boxes, everywhere Rae wasn't. They couldn't have failed to see the trail of wet footprints leading from the shower to the bed.

"Nice place," he remarked dryly.

Dry was underselling it. Everything about this man seemed to literally crackle with age, from his bony fingers to his dome of white hair, every part of him down to the thin slit in his face where his lips were supposed to be.

"Thanks," she said awkwardly, kicking a pair of Devon's pants discreetly out of sight as he finally turned to face her.

"With a view of the river to boot," he remarked. "I could never have afforded something like this at your age."

"Well, that was sometime in the late 1700s, wasn't it?" Rae answered in a voice as inflectionless as his. "They probably didn't have places like this back then."

It was rude, to be sure, but she saw absolutely no reason to pay him any sort of deference. This was the man who would see her in chains. Who had kept women like her in a position of second-hand prominence for the last sixty years, and who had kept hybrids like her on the run. As far as she was concerned he could take a swan dive from her penthouse balcony into the river.

"Forgive me if I find your impertinence hardly shocking, Miss Kerrigan," he said, wandering in a wide circle around the living room. "It's no less than what I've come to expect." He rested a withered hand on one of the boxes. "Still moving in, I see."

Rae gritted her teeth, furious with this man's intrusion into her house. "Well, up until recently we weren't sure whether or not we'd be returning."

"We? Ah, yes." His face cleared as he understood. "Yes, I saw Mr. Wardell leaving as I was just pulling up. He looked...a bit under the weather."

Rae stiffened. "He's fine."

For the first time, Victor offered a faint smile, patting the unopened boxes. "Still not sure, then? As to whether or not you'll return?"

She jutted up her chin, and he took her silence as his answer.

"Do you know what the President of the Privy Council does, Miss Kerrigan?" he asked, settling himself down in Molly's prized chair.

Her blood boiled at the sight but she reined in her anger, refusing to give him the satisfaction of seeing it. "I think the better question is do *you* know what the President of the Privy Council does, Mr. Mallins? Between the two of us, you're the one occupying the position."

His glittering black eyes fastened squarely on hers. "The job of the president is that of a servant. I am here merely to represent my constituents. To give a single voice to the masses. And to assist the people in those things they are incapable of doing themselves."

"So," she sneered, "you've come here to arrest me all on your own?"

"Don't be silly," he answered, pulling on a pair of black driving gloves. "I've come to take you out to lunch."

It has to be said Victor Mallins and Rae Kerrigan couldn't have made a more awkward pair.

It was a clash of the Titans. Old versus new. Young versus old. Modern versus...something that looked more at home in the time of Jack the Ripper.

In honor of the bright summer sun Rae had conjured herself a pair of tight-fitting white jeans along with a stunning turquoise camisole that laced up the sides and hung in bright ribbons down her bare back. Her hair was swept up in a stylish ponytail and long jeweled earrings dangled down to lightly touch her shoulders.

Normally she never took so much time to get ready, but seeing as Victor had no choice but to wait outside the door until she was finished, she decided to make the effort.

For his part, Victor could have stepped straight out of something written by Edgar Allen Poe. Despite the summer heat he wore strict, formal dress clothes: Black slacks, a white collared shirt, an ebony traveler's cloak, and a pair of leather riding gloves to top it off.

When they'd first walked outside, Rae half expected him to call his horse. He called his driver instead, and together the two of them headed down the street to a fancy Italian place Rae and Molly had yet to try.

The air conditioning had been turned all the way up and Rae shivered as they stepped inside, wondering if it was too late to duck back into the car and conjure herself a jacket.

Probably the reason he picked this place, she thought resentfully. *If I die of hypothermia before the cheese platter, then all his problems are solved.*

"Oh, Mr. Mallins!" A nervous-looking host hurried forward the second they walked inside. "We weren't expecting you today."

"That's quite alright, Billy," Victor took off his gloves and cloak and handed them to the young man, who hung them quickly on a coat rack.

No wonder the man acts like he's onboard the Titanic... everyone enables him!

The man shifted anxiously from foot to foot. "I'm so sorry, but since we didn't know you were coming your usual table is occupied. Perhaps you'd like to try something up on the..." His voice trailed off as old snake-eyes shot him a cold stare. "Actually, why don't I just ask the couple occupying the table to move? I'm sure they won't mind."

Victor didn't crack a smile. "That would be wonderful, Billy. Thank you."

'Billy' hurried off, mumbling so softly that Rae had to switch into Devon's tatù to hear, "I'm sure they won't mind at all. They're only on their *honeymoon...*"

"Nice place," Rae repeated Victor's words from earlier, hoping to fill up the awkward silence that followed the host's departure. As she glanced around she saw an elderly couple watching Victor from behind a potted plant beside their table. The look in their eyes was the same one as Billy's. Again, Rae shivered... Something that had nothing to do with the air conditioning.

Victor ignored her and waited without blinking for Billy to return. Moments later they were seated on the upper level of the restaurant, at a prime table centered in front of a huge floor-to-ceiling window. Billy had openly gawked when he noticed Rae's casual attire, staring between her and Victor like perhaps she was some street urchin who had followed him in. He blanched again when she seated herself without waiting for him to pull out her chair.

"Two iced teas to start," Victor instructed, opening his menu.

Rae hated iced tea. But she held her tongue and opened her menu as well, thanking the gods of fine dining that—curtesy of Princess Sarah's tatù—she spoke fluent Italian.

"So," she began conversationally, "why is it that everyone in here is so afraid of you? I mean, it's not like any of them know what you really do."

Victor kept his eyes glued to the menu. "Do you see that huge bank outside?"

Rae glanced out the window at the towering white Colonial sitting across the river. "The Danske? Of course."

"I own the bank."

Unable to think of a single thing to say to this, Rae nodded casually and lowered her face behind her menu.

Well, I'm sure I could conjure a bank. Just, give me a few years...

"Ah, Billy," Victor said the second the man returned. Although he was clearly labeled as a host, Rae got the feeling that because Victor had labeled him his 'go-to' guy, Billy doubled as a server when the banking mogul was in the building. "We'll have two coniglio cacciatore. Rare."

"Wait..." Rae glanced up in horror as Billy disappeared. "Coniglio, isn't that—"

"Rabbit. Yes."

A bunny rabbit. And of course he ordered it rare.

Her throat welled up as the six-year-old part of her started to silently cry, but she held it together on the outside and took a determined sip of her tea. "Why are we here, Victor?"

No more 'Mr. Mallins.' She decided it somewhere between the bank and the bunny.

He took a deliberate sip of his own drink before setting it thoughtfully down. "We're here, Miss Kerrigan, because like I said, I represent my constituents. And for whatever reason, my constituents have elected to offer you and your friends another chance of employment within the Privy Council. We are here because I'm doing everything in my power to try to understand any possible reasoning behind that decision."

The hair on the back of Rae's neck stood on end as her eyes narrowed. "First of all let's just drop the whole 'and my friends' gimmick. We both know you're talking about me and me alone."

"If it suits you." Victor shrugged carelessly. "For reasons beyond comprehension you have inspired a deep loyalty in the Privy Council's newest and finest. You can try to separate yourself in conversation all you wish, but you and I both know that the four of you come as a package deal. To talk about them is to talk about you. And vice versa."

"And you don't think I'm a worthy asset?"

"I think you live up to your *name*, Miss Kerrigan."

Little blue sparks danced at the tips of Rae's fingers and she was quick to hide them under the table. She would not let Victor see how much he—and this place—were rattling her.

He noticed anyway, taking it all in with bland interest as the plates of steaming rabbit were set in front of them. "Do you know why Guilder was established in the first place, Miss Kerrigan?" he asked, cutting off a slice of meat with a sudden flash of his knife.

Rae's eyes followed the movements as she hastened to recall her history. "Henry VIII knew about people with abilities, and established a safe place for them in the hopes that one of them could help him procure a son."

"That's right," Victor agreed, chewing slowly. "In fact, one could say that Guilder was a school set up for sons." He let the heavy implication hang in the air between them before moving on. "But that's the public reason for establishing the school. I'm talking about the practical reason."

The *practical* reason? Rae blanked.

Victor nodded to himself as he speared a carrot.

"The practical reason was so that when young people around the world turned sixteen and were gifted with unspeakable power they would have a safe place to learn how to use it. A place with instructors. A place with safety nets and boundaries. Somewhere they could test the limits of their gifts without fear of reprisal for themselves or anyone around them. It is a sacred privilege to teach there. An ancient responsibility to guard its gates and secrets." He took a swig of tea and stared at her carefully. "Tell me, Miss Kerrigan, can you think of anyone you and I both know who stands as a constant threat to all that?"

It took Rae a second to understand. Then she stared at him in shock. "*Me?*" she asked in astonishment. "You think I'm a threat to Guilder?"

Victor's face turned grim. "I think you bring dark things with you wherever you go. When you enter the sacred gates of Guilder, I think you bring them with you there."

Rae pushed back her plate in a rage. "I've done nothing, *nothing* but protect the students and secrets of Guilder since they were made aware to me. Protect them from *dark things* that you and your ancient, all-powerful association let slip inside undetected."

"Ah, yes, so you're talking about—"

"Lanford, Kraigan, Jennifer Jones. All people who not only infiltrated the population of Guilder, but you geniuses opened the gates and literally welcomed them inside."

"All people who were drawn there, because they were targeting *you*."

Rae slapped the table so hard some of her tea spilled. "All people who were drawn there because they were working for Jonathon Cromfield!"

Victor stared back at her calmly. "Who was also drawn to Guilder because he was targeting *you*."

Rae was so angry she was beginning to feel light-headed. She sucked in quick, silent gasps of air, but still she felt no relief. Was there no oxygen in this place? Were the air conditioning vents so strong they were literally sucking the life right out of it? "Are you..." She tried to find the words. "Are you blaming me for being a target?"

"Not at all," Victor said calmly, taking another bite. "I'm simply asking that you acknowledge you *are* one—and as such—let me ask you: Do you really want to place that same target on the backs of those people around you?"

She shook her head quickly back and forth, eyes darting almost subconsciously to the exits as she craved an end to this meeting. "Considering that your people voted to have me come back, you sure are doing a great job of trying to talk me out of it."

"I'm merely posing a question, Miss Kerrigan." He set down his fork and knife and leaned across the table so they were very close. Too close. She felt as though she could get lost forever in those cold, endless eyes. "If danger follows you wherever you go... why would you bring that danger here? To the place you call home? To the people you say you love?"

Before she realized what was happening, two silent tears slipped down her face. Victor calmly extended a handkerchief whilst simultaneously turning to Billy, who had just arrived.

"Splendid, Billy. I'd like to place an order for two plates of tiramisu."

Rae walked home slowly from the restaurant, clutching her takeout box of tiramisu. Victor had insisted she take it with her, and she had insisted that she walk. They'd both compromised, and went their separate ways at the door; one climbing back into his town car, the other making her way mournfully down the streets of London on foot, holding a box of fine Italian dessert.

When Victor had shown up at her door late that morning, she could honestly say that she wasn't worried for a single moment as to whether or not he could get to her. She was right, he was wrong. He was the bad guy, she was something else entirely. She didn't think his words could sting because she didn't think there was anything to them besides empty intimidation.

She could not have been more wrong.

The sun beat down on her bare shoulders as she trudged down the busy sidewalks, bumping into people now and then as she did.

When he phrased it like that... Not placing blame but simply recognizing a problem...

Wasn't he at least a little bit right?

She may not be dangerous but the people constantly coming after her were. Did it not then stand to reason that if she remained too close to any place or person in particular, that those precious things would also be at risk?

The most infuriating part of his argument was that it was the same internal battle she'd been having ever since Lanford locked her in that dungeon all those years ago. It was the same ledge that Devon and even Molly and Julian had to talk her down from time and time again.

But they were being loyal, and brave, and kind.

They weren't necessarily being *smart*.

Because of their association with her each one had suffered in turn. Beth had been banished to France and brainwashed. Julian had been mentally and physically assaulted more times than she could count—the most recent being Cromfield literally forcing his way inside Julian's head. Molly had been thrown into cars, dragged in circles around the globe, and held hostage with a gun to her head. Luke had been knocked into a coma. Gabriel had almost been killed. And Devon?

Devon had been kidnapped, tortured, beaten, bruised—anything and everything you could imagine. He had endured it all, for her. But perhaps the worst thing to happen to Devon was something none of them ever saw coming.

Hope.

A stubborn, damnable hope that he and Rae could have a normal life together. That if he could just pull them through all the darkness fate had thrown their way there was a light waiting for them there at the end.

That was the biggest hurt of all. Because there was no hope. Not when the man who was chasing her was immortal. Not when she was immortal herself.

She walked around the lovely little park that separated her house from Devon's several times, wondering on every pass if she should ring the front door and go inside. She could actually see Julian through the window—hair up in a ponytail, drinking a beer—as he slowly unloaded a trunk full of boxes. Devon's car was in the driveway as well. And again she was tempted.

It would be so easy.

She would just walk inside and tell both of them exactly what had happened. They would be appalled. They would be enraged. They would call Molly so that she could come and be appalled and enraged too. They would tear Victor to shreds. Trash his argument. Trash his character. They would never, for a single second, acknowledge that anything he said might be true. And they would never, for a single second, even consider taking his advice and keeping their distance.

She would be cheered. She would be comforted. And the whole thing would be forgotten.

Yes, it would be very easy.

But...it wouldn't exactly be true.

She walked past one more time before finally giving up and heading home. Her eyes swam with a hundred forbidden tears as she marched dejectedly into her lobby, past the over-enthusiastic attendant—Raphael—who glanced up from his phone with a look of concern. He leapt immediately from his chair but she merely held up a hand and headed straight towards the elevator.

She didn't have the strength to comfort him right now. Not when she felt like she was falling apart at the seams.

The elevator shot her to the top floor and she climbed out wearily, dragging her feet as she dropped her purse to the ground with a *thud*.

At least no one is here, she thought miserably. She'd have until Devon showed up at dinner to wallow in her grief.

She was about to kick off her heels and do exactly that when she suddenly realized that the shower was running. It was coming from her bathroom, not Molly's, and she ghosted lightly down the hall to investigate.

The second she heard the sound, she had to admit a part of her was relieved. Smart as it may be, she didn't want to think about what Victor said another moment. She wanted to be comforted by her friends, held by her boyfriend. She wanted to close her eyes and have everything be okay.

Even if it really wasn't...

"What did you do," she pushed open the door with a grin, preparing to strip down and join her boyfriend for round two, "spill more orange juice?"

Then the man in the shower turned around.

A man who was certainly not Devon.

She dropped her tiramisu on the floor.

"What gives, Kerrigan?" Gabriel said with a grin. "Can't you knock?"

Chapter 11

"Gabriel! What-the-hell-are-you-doing-here!"

Rae was in such a state that all the words strung themselves together. She didn't know where to look or where not to look. Her eyes shot down to her dessert—puddling on the floor, to the steam—billowing down from over the open glass doors, and finally to her own petrified expression in the mirror—pale and teary-eyed.

There was a shift of movement in the corner of her eye, and all at once Gabriel was standing right in front of her. Dripping wet. Unapologetically naked.

She snapped her eyes shut with a stifled profanity.

"Since you seem exceptionally unobservant today, I'll tell you," he said. She could hear the smile in his voice. "I'm taking a shower."

He leaned in even closer as she froze on the spot, her mind reeling as she tried to think of how to make the most graceful escape. However, simply too many things had happened since she got up this morning. Her emotionally whiplashed brain couldn't seem to settle on a single thing except: *freeze.*

The heat and moisture from his body soaked through her thin shirt, and in addition to closing her eyes she covered them with a hand. "And is there a reason you had to leave your hotel to come and take a shower here?" she demanded, groping the air behind her for the door.

"I was lonely. Figured I'd come over and say hi."

"You were lonely," she repeated through gritted teeth. She eventually gave up on finding the door handle and simply stepped blindly in the general direction. "Well let me tell you—"

But in her haste to escape she had forgotten one critical thing. The tiramisu.

As one foot landed squarely on top of it at the same time the other slid out from under her completely. She fell towards the slippery ground with a stifled shriek. Except she never got there.

Two strong, wet arms caught her instead.

"Gabriel!" she shouted, finally opening her eyes.

By now the steam and splashing of the shower had completely soaked through her clothes and hair—a condition that wasn't helped much seeing as how he was holding her against his naked body.

He grinned down at her, still holding her down in a dip. Little drops of water flew off the tips of his hair and landed in hers as his green eyes sparkled with mischief. "What? Did you want me to let you fall? Not very gentlemanly..."

"You're naked!" she cried, trying and failing to pull away.

"You're clumsy," he fired back, shaking his head with a sympathetic smile. "We all have our crosses to bear."

"Oh, I know exactly how you meant that! Please! Get off of me!"

"Fine." Without any kind of ceremony, he dropped her where she stood.

That would have been all well and good had she been standing, but as things were she fell straight down atop the smeared chocolate-coffee monstrosity that had become her nightmare.

"Oh..." Gabriel winced as she lay there not moving, not bothering to get up. "Okay, *truth*? I honestly forgot about that when I let you go."

She still didn't move. She just lay there, covering her face with her hands as the weight of the day came crashing down upon her.

"Rae? Honey?" he tried again. There was the sound of splashing water as he knelt down beside her. "I'm sorry about your dessert. And your clothes. You're not...you're not paralyzed or in shock or something, are you?"

A pair of warm fingers pinched her leg, and she flinched.

"Nope, not paralyzed." More splashing and shifting. "Uh, you want to get up now? Or...at least give me some clue as to what's going on? I said I was sor—"

He stopped short as she sat bolt upright, tears streaming freely down her face.

"Shit, Rae! Are you hurt or—"

Her hands scrunched up into angry little fists and she literally pounded the tiles beside them in a helpless, kitten sort of rage.

"Why do you...just...have to ruin everything!?"

Then she lost it. Completely lost it. She couldn't remember the last time she cried so hard. She couldn't breathe. She couldn't think. She couldn't do anything except just sit there, bury her face in her hands, and wait for it all to be done.

After a couple of minutes Gabriel seemed to realize that this couldn't possibly be entirely about him. He turned down the water to the bath setting, wrapped his waist in a towel, and lifted her slowly to sit on the edge of the tub. She kinda missed getting a better glimpse of his bare, muscular bottom.

Then without further ado, he grabbed a washcloth and began gently wiping the bits of chocolate and coffee from her ruined shirt. She didn't even realize what he was doing until he'd finished with the shirt and moved on to her foot. She was crying that hard.

"What—" she pulled away with another broken sob, "what are you doing?"

He smiled softly and took it back in his hand, gently rubbing it clean. "One day, Rae Kerrigan, I'm going to show you the proper way to eat an Italian dessert."

She laughed breathlessly, wiping tears from her face. "I'm sorry, I didn't mean to just fall apart on—"

"Don't be," he interrupted quietly. "I get it. You're going through a lot right now." His eyes traced her face with kind sympathy. "You want to talk about it?"

Her breath caught in her chest and she shook head quickly back and forth, more tears spilling down her neck.

"Okay," he said quickly, squeezing her foot before he placed it back in the warm water. As the tub reached critical mass, he flicked off the water and perched on the edge beside her, dangling his legs in the water beside hers. "You want to just sit here a while?"

More tears fell as she bit her lip and nodded.

"Okay," he murmured again, placing a hesitant arm around her back. "We can just sit here then. We can sit here as long as you like..."

They sat a very long while. Long enough for the hot water to turn cold. After about five minutes or so of constant quiet sobbing, Rae had given up all pretenses and had laid her head on his bare chest. He'd complied instantly, wrapping both arms around her and pulling her gently onto his lap so he could hold her more securely. After six minutes she'd even forgotten that all he was wearing was a thin towel.

After a while, though, the tears subsided and the freezing water was enough to start Rae shivering. Without saying a word Gabriel reached down to pull the drain on the tub before twisting behind himself to grab her another towel.

"Thanks," she murmured, wrapping it around both shoulders. In hindsight, she had no idea why she'd spent the last who-knows-how-long dangling her legs in a bathtub when she was still wearing white skinny jeans.

She looked down in dismay, and Gabriel chuckled softly. "You can take them off," he turned immediately to face the other way, "I won't look." She froze uncertainly, and he chuckled again. "Come on, Rae, you've got to be cold."

She was cold. And still dripping wet.

As quickly as she could, she stripped off the soaking jeans and threw them in a pile in the corner. Her shirt landed on top. Only then, once she was securely in a towel of her own, did she clear her throat awkwardly.

"Okay, I'm...um...I'm dressed. Ish."

Gabriel turned around with a twinkle in his eyes. "Beautiful."

She blushed and sighed all at once. "Why do you always do that?"

He threw up his hands in genuine innocence. "Rae, for once, I swear I'm not doing—"

But then her face crumbled and she collapsed into tears once more.

He registered the change with a look of horror and gathered her immediately up in his arms. "I'm sorry again. Rae, I'm sorry! I didn't mean anything by it, I swear. You're actually just really, really pretty. I didn't mean to—"

No matter what he said it wouldn't have made a difference. The second he'd thrown up his arms, Rae had seen the fading remains of a horrific abrasion he'd suffered at the hands of Cromfield. An abrasion he'd suffered...because of her.

"Victor Mallins came to see me this morning," she sobbed, burying her face in his chest.

Every muscle stiffened in rage. "Victor Mallins?"

"He made me eat a bunny."

At this point Gabriel froze, tilting his head down to look at her in sheer bewilderment. "Okay, I know I don't have your boyfriend's tatù, so I couldn't have heard that right. He made you eat a—"

"And then he told me I'm responsible for every bad thing that's ever happened to anyone who's ever been around me!"

"But, Rae," he tilted her chin up and tried to coax a smile, "that's crazy—"

"*No, it isn't!*" she cried. "*It's true!*" Her whole body seemed to collapse against him as she lost herself to her tears.

His hands, tentative at first, soon grew bolder, wrapping tightly around her body; one on her lower back, one on her head. He soothed and calmed, squeezing her tightly and whispering comfortingly into her hair. But still she cried.

When she was finally able to catch her breath, she tried again. "It's absolutely t-true! I have this g-giant target on my b-back. Whoever I g-get close to, they get it t-too!"

"Rae, please," he put both hands on the side of her face, "just calm down a second."

"No, Gabriel. C-Can't you see?! When Cromfield beat you— that was me. And Molly. And Jules. And Devon. My m-mom. All of you! The only reason a-any of these bad things happen is because you're close to m-me!"

He stared down steadily into her eyes. "I don't believe that for a second. And I don't think you really do either. If you weren't around, if you were never even born into the picture, Cromfield would still be after hybrids. He'd still eventually come to Guilder. He'd still infiltrate the Council."

"I know that, I just—" She pushed her hair back and stared up tearfully into his eyes. "I just don't want anyone to get hurt, you know? Not because of me."

His face softened. "They won't. If anything, you being here has diverted his attention from people who might not be able to stand up under the pressure."

She couldn't help but laugh sarcastically, still collapsed against him as he supported nearly all of her weight. "Yeah, because I'm so clearly able to stand up under it myself."

He smiled fondly. "Maybe not tonight. But tonight you don't have to be. Tonight you have m—" he caught himself quickly, "all of us."

All of us.

Rae considered the words as she caught her breath and tried to pull herself together. "You know," her voice was low and scratchy from crying, "I was actually surprised you were able to come with us. That Carter let you. I don't know what you said to him, but—"

"I didn't say anything." Gabriel pulled in a rather shaky breath of his own. "I let him use his tatù on me."

Rae's mouth fell open. "You did?"

She couldn't imagine how hard that must have been—for the both of them. Carter saw firsthand every lie, every betrayal. Then again, he also saw all the steps that led to Gabriel's eventual transformation. The moment he turned his back on Cromfield and chose to side with Guilder. But for Gabriel there was no greater invasion than Carter's tatù. It was something that Rae had both used and had used against her, so she knew perfectly well the amount of trust it must have required for Gabriel to have willingly volunteered himself. Just to clear his name.

She remembered when Devon had done the same thing just a few months ago. He'd offered to let Carter peer into his very soul, all to justify his feelings for Rae.

It was a complete surrender that could never be taken lightly. Could never be done without one's consent. And even then could only be done with the utmost care.

It was also Rae's greatest secret.

That she had done it to Gabriel in his sleep.

There was no malice behind it at all. She'd simply had to understand. Had to understand how he could have completely betrayed her trust and then turned right around and saved her life.

He didn't know she'd done it, and she'd never told him. Never told him that she'd seen his entire life story in a single instant. Never told him that she knew he loved her.

"Which as you know is a big deal, right, Rae?"

His eyes flashed up to hers and her heart stopped cold in her chest. What exactly was he saying? This wasn't the first time he'd done something like this. Except...he couldn't know, could he? After a second she realized she wasn't even breathing.

But he held her gaze for only a moment before his face melted into an easy smile. "After all, he did it to you, right?"

She exhaled in a shaky sigh. "Yeah. He...that was... I can't believe you did that, Gabriel."

"Well it was the only way to clear my name," he said with a tight smile. "Even if it wasn't the most *desirable* one."

She shook her head sympathetically, still trying to wrap her mind around it. "Why was it even so important to you what Carter—"

Then his lips were on hers.

She couldn't think. Couldn't move. Couldn't breathe.

His lips were soft, but strong. Practiced, but playful. They eased hers open before she even knew it, and the kiss deepened.

And what a kiss. Damn, he was good!

He kissed so differently than Devon.

Devon was strong as well, but sweet. Thoughtful. Every movement, every gesture—it was always done with her in mind.

Gabriel was a bit of a wild card.

The next second he threw her up against the wall, tangling his fingers roughly through her damp hair and tilting her head up to his. How he was doing all of this considering he still had broken ribs, Rae would never know. But he did it, and he did it well.

It was only then that she realized she was kissing him back.

"Wh—?!"

There was a burst of lightening and he went flying backwards across the hall, landing with a painful gasp somewhere in Molly's room. Before he could even get up she had flown across the apartment and was towering over him in a rage.

"What the hell do you think you're doing!" She clutched her towel firmly to her chest, relieved beyond measure that his had managed to stay on as well.

He panted as he caught his breath, pulling himself cautiously up to his feet while watching her with a roguish grin. "Again— exceptionally unobservant, Kerrigan. I was kissing you."

Rae's skin flushed simultaneously hot and cold. "And why the hell would you go and do something like that?! When I'm with someone!"

He only grinned wider. "I think the real question is, if you're with someone," he leaned in so they were just inches away, "why the hell did you kiss me back?"

Blue fire exploded from her hands and he jumped a step away. "*Oh, you little—*"

But just then the door opened and slammed shut as the sound of other shouting voices suddenly filled the apartment.

"Oh shit," Rae breathed, freezing in place, "that's Molly and Luke."

Gabriel grimaced. "Take it their breakfast date didn't go well."

Her eyes flickered down to both of them, still half naked, and she grabbed his arm with a hiss. "What are we supposed to do?!"

"Well...we could always put on a little show."

"I'm going to actually kill you."

"Yeah?" He laughed silently. "Then you'll have to explain why you dragged a naked corpse into your best friend's room, instead of just a naked man."

Rae hands balled into fists. "You have no idea how utterly infuriating you—"

The raging voices headed their way, and instead of finishing her sentence Rae yanked Gabriel down on the other side of the bed. They cowered there together, one beside the other as Molly and Luke stormed into the room and slammed the door.

"—just don't understand how you're somehow okay with it!" Luke was saying. Yelling was more like it. Rae had never heard him so upset.

Molly was just as enraged. "I'm *okay* with it because it's over now! Yeah, I didn't expect to get suddenly trapped in a long-distance relationship for a month either, but what was I supposed to do? Let her go by herself?!"

Rae turned to Gabriel with a wince, slipping into her telepathy. *See? My fault.*

He grinned and spoke so softly that only Rae with her tatù could hear him. "Yeah, I'd have to agree with you on that one."

She elbowed him sharply in the ribs and he fell silent.

"No, I'm not saying you let her go by herself; I'm just saying when are you and I going to become the priority?" Luke was pacing back and forth now, a look of sheer frustration darkening his handsome face. "I'd wait an eternity for you, Skye, you know that. But I have to know that things are at least moving in a more normal direction."

"*More normal?*" Molly shrieked. "*More normal* is the only thing I've been trying so hard to do here! You should have seen me this morning! I basically punched Julian in the face when he tried to use his powers. Why the hell do you think I got this apartment in the first place?"

Luke glanced around at the crown moldings. "Because you're vain?"

Gabriel grinned again and whispered, "I like him."

Molly tossed back her flaming hair. "That *and* because I want to have a 'normal life' more than anything I've ever wanted in the whole world. Normal, with a healthy dose of super-spy. I don't think it's too much to ask."

"It isn't too much to ask," he paced forward, gripping her hands, "but I've no idea what, if any part of that, includes me! You take off for a month and a half with no word—"

"I *told* you, Devon smashed my phone!"

"And Rae couldn't have conjured you a new one?"

It was a fair point. But with one little hitch...

"So that the call could have been traced back and Cromfield and his minions could have come after you?" Molly shot back. "I don't think so!"

Rae nodded resoundingly. *You go girl!*

Gabriel, meanwhile, was shaking his head. And it seemed Luke shared his sentiments.

"How am I supposed to protect you when you disappear in the middle of the night and don't even leave a note letting me know where you are?"

"Luke," she sighed, "I can protect myself—"

"I know! You with your lightning hands! All your friends and your damn powers! That's not what I'm talking about, Molly, and you know it! I'm talking about *you*. How am I supposed to be there for you, when—"

"You can be there for me now! I'm back! We have no plans to go anywhere else anytime soon! I have this apartment, we're together! Everything is finally okay—"

"Everything is *not* finally okay because I LOVE YOU!"

The room went dead quiet.

Rae clapped her hands over her mouth.

Gabriel nodded appreciatively and mouthed the word 'smooth.'

"You..." For the first time since Rae had met her, Molly was stunned. "You what?"

There was the sound of ruffling clothes as Luke brought them both together. "I love you, dummy." He grinned. "What, you have to make me say it twice?"

Grabbing Gabriel's hand and turning them both invisible, Rae peeked over the side of the bed with a huge, trespassing smile.

Molly was smiling just as brightly. "I'm going to make you say it all the time."

He scooped her up and kissed her on the tip of the nose. "Is that right?"

"Oh yes," she giggled. "In the morning, in the afternoon. In a Scottish accent..."

"I love you, Molly Skye," Luke did his best impersonation.

Rae and Gabriel shook their heads at the same time, while Molly snorted with laughter.

"Okay—never again in an accent."

Luke grinned, pressing his face up against hers as he kissed her again and again. "Yeah, but I can keep saying it, right? You think you might say it back to me anytime soon?"

Molly erupted in another fit of giggles as he lowered her down onto the bed. "I love you too, Luke. Accent or no. I love you."

Rae clapped her hand over her heart and Gabriel rolled his eyes.

"You know," Luke stretched up and pulled his shirt over his head, before lowering himself back down on top of her. "I could get used to hearing that. I love to see you naked also."

Rae realized in horror where this was all leading. She glanced in panic at the closed door. While they could certainly make it there unseen, they couldn't open it without both people knowing. And from the way things were heating up on the bed she and Gabriel needed to get out of there—quick!

She couldn't remove her invisible cloak to use the telepathy, so she merely tugged on Gabriel's arm to get his attention and pointed to the floor. Hopefully he got the hint.

"Hey...Molls?" she called tentatively.

There was a bright blue explosion as Molly screamed, and electricity shot to all four corners of the room.

"WHAT THE HELL'S GOING ON?"

Rae switched back to living color, lifting one hand in surrender over her head while the other clutched fearfully at her towel. "Heeeeeey, bestie. So, anyway, that was a lovely chat you guys had. Luke, you did a great job and now we're just going to go so that you two can—"

"Rae Kerrigan! You get back here this instant!" Molly screamed, holding up Luke's jacket in front of her chest as Rae and Gabriel went tearing from the room.

"Have fun!"

"Use protection!" Gabriel added as a vase burst over his head.

They raced across the apartment to the front door, flinching as occasional bursts of electricity fired their way.

"Are things always this dramatic in your life?" Gabriel gasped with a breathless smile, pulling on his pants with one hand and groping for the door with another.

"Oh no," Rae lied, grinning from ear to ear as she yanked a hastily-conjured dress over her head and dropped the towel. "Normally things are super quiet!"

Then she yanked open the door and her jaw fell straight to the floor.

"Super quiet, huh?" Angel grinned and struck a pose. "That's not what I've heard..."

Chapter 12

"Angie?"

For a split second it didn't matter that Gabriel was standing in nothing but a pair of gorgeous jeans that hugged his hips in all the right places. It didn't matter that he looked like some kind of sex god on the run from the lightning storm still shooting from Molly's room. All at once he was a five-year-old kid again. Five years old, and staring at his long-lost sister.

There was a blur of white and blond, and then they were in each other's arms.

Rae watched a bit awkwardly from the door frame, feeling as though she was intruding upon some kind of family moment. When Luke and Molly came tearing from the room they, too, stopped abruptly short and gawked at the pair before swiftly averting their eyes.

"Gabriel, I..." Angel leaned back in shock, hands on both of his cheeks as she frantically searched his eyes. "I didn't think there was any way in hell I'd ever see you in this place. What are you...?" For a split second she looked abruptly afraid. "What exactly are you doing here?"

"Relax; it's okay," Gabriel murmured, unwilling to let her go. "It seems I had the same little existential revelation that you apparently had in San Francisco." This time it was he who leaned back, fixing her in an accusatory stare. "You know, when you *faked your own death.*"

He was a serious as Rae had ever seen him. As serious, and as thoughtful, and as caring, and as concerned. There was nothing but pure emotion as he looked down at Angel. No walls, no jokes, no games. It was something deeper than that—something pure.

Although Rae knew there was nothing but a fierce familial bond between them, that they were nothing more than orphaned siblings, an irrational part of her couldn't help but feel the faintest tug of jealousy.

First you kiss him back, and now you're jealous? What the hell's wrong with you Kerrigan?

The faintest hint of a blush appeared in Angel's pale, porcelain skin as she saw the hurt on her brother's face. "But how could I tell you?" she asked, her blue eyes as wide as saucers. "I knew how you felt about them. How you felt about..." Her voice trailed off as she seemed to notice Rae for the first time. There was a rather ironic pause, and Rae was suddenly sure Angel had been about to say her name. But as soon as Angel saw her she gave her a curious once-over, before returning to Gabriel—eyes sparkling with sudden mischief as she simultaneously realized that he was not wearing a shirt.

"It seems I have a bit to catch up on."

"Yeah! We *all* need to sit down and have a long talk," Molly interrupted, breaking the touching family moment. She shot Rae a vicious glare as she and Luke wandered over, before giving Angel the obligatory welcoming nod. "It's, um, weird to see you again, Angel."

"Likewise." Angel grinned, finally peeling herself off of Gabriel as her eyes swept the rest of the room. "Is Julian here?"

"No, I'm afraid not. But he's not far, though. He bought a house about four minutes down the street," Rae explained, wondering for the first time what Julian's reaction might be, or whether or not he even knew Angel was coming. Although he never talked about it openly, Rae knew he missed her to an almost painful degree. That being said, he had told her to keep her distance for a good reason—it wasn't safe for her here.

Molly's eyes flashed electric fire. "That's right. He bought a house with *Devon*."

Gabriel's head jerked up at the name while Rae dropped hers immediately. For her part, Molly continued to glare at Rae with the strength of a million suns.

Angel glanced between the two feuding girls before hopping up on the kitchen counter with a look of blatant glee. "It seems I've come at an interesting time."

Rae shifted nervously on her feet, doing her best to avoid Molly's savage stare while not being obvious about it. "Oh, not really." She added quickly, "Do you want me to text Jules? I can't believe he wasn't here to meet you."

"He didn't know I was coming," Angel said with a mischievous smile. Then her face softened as she considered. "And no, don't text him. I'm sure he'll be around soon enough and I'd love to surprise him."

"Aw," Molly smiled sweetly, before turning the same saccharine smile to Rae, "the day's just been full of surprises. Hasn't it, Rae?"

Angel laughed, a light, sparkling sound that somehow reminded Rae very much of Gabriel. "Okay, what happened? Did Rae kill your dog or something?"

Molly jutted up her chin with a sniff. "It's so, *so* much worse than that."

"On that note..." Gabriel turned to Luke for the first time. "I'm Gabriel, by the way. Really like your style, man. And your hair."

Rae noticed the hair at the same time. It had grown out quite a bit since being half-shaved down for the surgery following his coma. Now it looked like something vaguely resembling a modern, stylish mohawk. Nothing too flashy, but unique. And undeniably cool. And the way it angled down around his handsome face? Rae had to admit she fully approved.

Luke shook his hand, looking both self-conscious and confused. "Uh...thanks."

For a minute the lot of them just stood there. There was so much to say, that no one could seem to think of anything to say at all. It had just reached the point of becoming unbearably awkward when the clock chimed seven and there was a prompt knock at the door.

Devon and her dinner date! Rae paled—she had completely forgotten.

Determined not to look anywhere in Molly's general direction, she broke the silent circle to open the door once more. As she did so she made a mental note to just bolt the damn thing shut. She couldn't handle any more surprises from it after today.

Both Devon and Julian were standing on the other side. Both dressed in casual dining clothes. Both looking adorably apologetic.

"Hey, babe," Devon kissed her on the cheek, eyes already searching for forgiveness, "so I know I said that you and I could do a special dinner tonight, just the two of us—but Julian didn't have anywhere to go and I couldn't just leave him alone at the house."

Julian looked at her with wide, serious eyes. "There's no telling what kind of shenanigans I might get up to."

Devon shot him a look then turned beseechingly back to Rae. "Do you think maybe he could join us? Before you answer," he held up two bottles in each hand, "I've got wine!"

Unable to answer, Rae simply opened the door the rest of the way with her foot. Devon's eyes widened as they fell on the crowd standing behind her. "It appears I should have brought a few more bottles..." he murmured.

Before he could say anything else Julian pushed past him, white as a sheet.

"Angel! What're you doing here?"

Instead of racing into his arms like she did with Gabriel, Angel kept her distance, sliding slowly off the counter and approaching at half-speed. "I heard you'd bought a house in

London. Thought I should stop by and check it out." She meant it to be coy, but Julian said nothing and she dropped the nervous act. "You wrote me a few days ago that Cromfield said he was going underground. Now, you may not know what that means, but I do." She and Gabriel shared a swift look. "It's rather literal. It means that he'll be completely out of touch with the rest of the world, and, as such, he's no real threat right now to anyone."

Julian looked like he was aching to reach for her, but a paralyzing fear was keeping him at bay. "And?" he asked stiffly, his voice almost too quiet to hear.

"And then I heard Jennifer Jones was dead."

Again, Angel looked at Gabriel for confirmation and received the slightest of nods in return.

A fleeting shadow flitted across her lovely face—as if she'd stepped momentarily out of the sun—before she looked up with a smile unrivaled by anything they had seen so far. "When I left the hotel in San Francisco, you said you'd be willing to..." She hesitated, scanning Julian's face with frightful uncertainty. "I didn't know if you were just saying that or... But the point is, it's safe now for me to be here if you wanted to—"

Rae had never seen Julian move so fast.

There was a blur of colors followed by a muffled collision.

Then Angel was up in the air. Wrapped in Julian's arms, gasping for breath as he kissed her with a strength and passion Rae had only seen on the cover of romance novels or on television.

For the second time that day Rae smiled to herself and politely averted her eyes as another of her best friends in the whole world was finally reunited with their one true love.

It had been a statistical nightmare, one of the rockiest roads of them all, and without a doubt—it had been a *long* time coming.

As she glanced covertly around the circle, she saw similar expressions on the faces of all her friends. Even Luke looked sincerely touched. Julian deserved this, possibly more than anyone else she knew. And from what she knew about Angel, she deserved something like this too.

Only Molly was staring openly at the couple, a stranger to manners. But her look of girlish happiness soon soured with a hint of distaste. "Okay, you guys...time to get a room."

Julian laughed aloud and pulled away, still holding onto Angel like she was a part of his own body. "Sorry," he gasped breathlessly though he looked like he was considering doing just that.

Gabriel flashed Angel a similar look of disapproval, but it was ruined by his grin.

For her part, Angel was in no hurry to be put down. But she stroked a long finger down the side of Julian's face, reading his eyes in a way that made Rae wonder if she also possessed telepathy, before she wriggled her way to the ground with a dancing smile.

"No, we need a little normal. Let's eat." She turned to Devon. "You said you have wine?"

"Uh...yeah," Devon answered, happy for his friend but a little off-balance by the speed at which everything was happening. After all, the last time Devon had seen Angel he'd openly threatened to kill her. He tried to catch Julian's eye, but with Angel in the room he didn't stand a chance. Instead, he just gestured to the long kitchen table with a heartfelt smile. "Shall we? Looks like we've got a lot to celebrate!"

"I'll say," Rae echoed, casually taking a seat as far away from Gabriel as possible.

"And I'm sure we're all going to need more than a little wine," Molly muttered, elbowing Devon deliberately out of the way so that she could sit on Rae's other side. "Gabriel, can you please put a shirt on?"

Rae stiffened, but hung her head when he left the room for a moment before returning to his seat by Angel. Rae was going to have to deal with her best friend sooner or later. The problem was that she had a sneaking suspicion that Molly was far less concerned with the fact that Rae happened to be in her room when she was about to have sex with Luke than she was that Rae happened to be in there with Gabriel. Naked. Well—in towels, but Rae was sure that Molly would write that off as naked. On the one hand, she supposed it was for the best that they just got it over with, considering that for the first time in his life her boyfriend was relatively deaf. On the other hand, dinner was probably not the best time...

For his part, Devon was completely oblivious to the tension emanating between the two, probably subconsciously writing it off as some sort of wardrobe or feng shui disagreement. He busied himself with unpacking the Chinese food he'd brought without another thought.

"Babe, could you conjure a few more bottles of wine?" he asked as he carried the take-out cartons to the table. He added to himself, "Thank goodness we got so much food..."

As Rae conjured a dozen more bottles, avoiding Molly's piercing stare all the while, Luke leaned across the table with genuine interest, staring between Gabriel and Angel.

"So, how is it that you two know each other?"

Still half-intertwined with Julian, Angel shot Gabriel a quick smile. "We grew up together."

"Oh, that's cool..." Luke smiled politely but then trailed off, glancing uncertainly at Molly. "Wait, I thought you said that Angel was—"

"Allow me to clarify," Gabriel took over, "we grew up together...with Cromfield."

Luke's eyebrows shot up and his eyes flickered around the table, apparently searching for some sort of 'just kidding!' When he didn't get one he seemed abruptly determined to remain as polite as possible, repeating his original phrase with his best attempt at normalcy.

"Oh, that's...cool."

"Wine?" Gabriel offered with a sympathetic grin.

"Please."

Several bottles popped open at once, and Rae sank an inch or two lower in her chair.

It was going to be one hell of a long night...

With a speed that was perhaps unwise, the seven friends emptied each of the bottles on the table. The more they drank, the more they relaxed, and, therefore, the more they talked. Jokes were told, bonds were forged. Stories that were, perhaps, best kept secret came tumbling into light, with both hilarious and often times disastrous effects.

"—and that's when he flew."

Angel slammed her hands down on the table. "He did not!"

"He did," Julian laughed. "Flew out with her in his arms. It was like something out of a movie. But like...a movie where the guy isn't that great at it yet, so he ends up getting hurt..."

"I thought you didn't really *fly*," Gabriel interjected, eyes gleaming at Devon over his raised wine glass. "I thought you just jumped really high."

"Semantics!" Molly cried. "He still *jumped off a cliff* to save her. And then jumped BACK UP AGAIN!" Although only half the table understood the reason, Molly had been particularly complimentary of Devon over the course of the meal. Increasingly more so the more she drank.

"And that's enough for you..." Rae tried to remove her glass, with no success.

"That's right," Gabriel continued, still looking at Devon with the same fixed stare, "that's why you were in such bad shape that you actually dropped her while trying to break her out of that secret chamber back at Guilder."

"Gabriel," Angel said sharply, "shut up and drink your wine."

She was the only person Rae had ever heard chide Gabriel besides herself. Circumstances aside, she kind of loved it.

"At least I didn't force myself on her while she was passed out on a fishing boat," Devon fired back, his eyes flashing. "Yeah—I know about that."

Gabriel leaned back with a cocky grin. "Semantics."

Luke sighed and emptied another bottle. "Your friends are so weird..." he said to Molly.

"No," Angel hiccupped, "the cliff-jumping thing—that's actually kind of sweet." She turned to Devon with a speculative smile. "You know, when you had me strapped down in that chair I thought you might be sweet underneath it all. You were so protective of Jules."

"*That's* what you took from that whole interrogation session?" Julian asked incredulously, gawking at her in disapproval. "That Devon was *sweet*?"

"Must be losing my touch," Devon muttered.

She shrugged carelessly. "I've been interrogated by worse."

"Seriously..." Luke said again, "...so freaking weird."

"*Changing the subject,*" Angel diverted them, sweeping back her sheet of white hair, "how's this new house the two of you bought together? Rae said it was just down the street?"

"Oh yeah," Rae piped up. "How did the unpacking go today? The two of you get a lot done?"

"The *two* of us?" Julian's forehead creased in a frown. "It was actually just—"

"We got a ton unloaded and set up," Devon cut him off quickly. Julian cast him the briefest of looks before clearing his face and pouring himself another glass of wine. "I think you girls are really going to like it. And, no, Molls," he interrupted her rant before it could even begin, "you can't be in charge of decorating."

The pint-sized redhead leaned back in her chair with a pout. "You know, sometimes I think you and I are making such progress, and then—*bam*! You say something like that..."

"Well you can help me decorate *my* new place," Gabriel volunteered. "I put in an offer on a studio just this morning."

Between the wine and the need for interior design, Molly actually forgot about her issues with him for a split second and leaned forward with unbearable excitement. "You did? Where? Can I seriously help?"

Gabriel leaned back in his chair, looking very pleased with himself. "Right here. In the very next building, in fact." His eyes flickered to Rae's. "I wanted to be close to all the action..."

A deep crimson blush flowered in Rae's cheeks, and she pushed back her chair—eager to end the meal as quickly as possible. "Well, I can't believe I ate so much food—I'm stuffed!" she said, crossing her arms over her stomach. "Off to bed, I think..."

"Not so fast." Devon got up and threw her a little wink. "I stopped by the new Italian place you and Molly have wanted to try and picked up some dessert." He rifled around in a near-empty container before pulling out several smaller boxes. "How do you feel about tiramisu?"

Rae spat a mouthful of wine across the table.

The others jerked back as the red stain spread slowly towards them. Only Gabriel remained where he was, eyes dancing as he grinned down at his lap.

"Babe?" Devon asked cautiously. "You okay?"

Rae froze in her chair, utterly humiliated, utterly mortified all at the same time. "What? Yes—I'm fine. Sorry! Just...went down the wrong pipe."

Angel gave her a curious look before heading to the kitchen. "I'll get some napkins to clean this up." Luke and Julian went to help her, while Devon began plating up the dessert.

Molly in the meantime turned to Rae with a whispered hiss. "You are SO lucky Angel happened to show up, because otherwise you'd have a LOT of explaining to do!"

Rae rolled her eyes and lowered her voice as well. "Molls, it's not what you think—"

"Oh really? It's not what I think?" Molly pulled back and gave her a stern look. "Then let me tell you what I know. Because all I *know* is that you and Gabriel were in my room together. *Naked*!"

"Naked?"

Everyone in the kitchen stopped cold.

Devon had paused by the plates with one hand still raised in the air, looking at Rae like he'd never seen her before.

"You and Gabriel?"

It was like all the air in the room had gone cold.

Julian, Angel, and Luke averted their eyes, and even Gabriel had the decency to lower his stare to the table. But Rae couldn't tear her eyes away from Devon.

She tried to answer several times but her windpipe locked down, and she went white as a sheet. Eventually, she managed a small, "Dev..."

His face was hard as a statue. Not a hint of emotion upon it.

"Like I said, we have a lot to celebrate." His eyes never left hers. "I got my tatù back today; Kraigan must have taken another. Perfect timing, huh?"

Ice-cold tears started running down Rae's face as she pushed herself up from the table.

"Devon, I can explain this—"

He held up a hand and she fell silent. "You know what, Rae?" Their eyes locked again and it felt like something died.

"I don't think you can..."

Chapter 13

Devon had certainly gotten his tatù back. He was out the door before Rae could even blink. Her hands came up to her face in what felt like slow motion as she stared after him, unable to move.

What have I done?

Then all at once the kitchen became a flood of movement.

Both Molly's hands clamped over her mouth with a look of pure horror, and she swiveled around in her chair to Rae. "Oh my goodness, Rae! I thought he still couldn't hear me. I had no idea he could! I just wanted you to tell me what was going on with Gabriel; I would *never* have said anything if I'd known—"

How did I let this happen? How could I let it happen?

Rae muttered inside her head on a continual loop, her eyes unfocused as she continued to stare out the open door. She was vaguely aware of the fact that people were still talking to her and things were still happening, but she couldn't get over those two little phrases over and over again. Was this how her father felt when her mom caught him?

"Go after him," Luke knelt at her other side, reasoning with her gently. "If it was me, I'd go after him."

How did I let this happen?

"What was that?" Luke turned to Molly with concern. "What did she say?"

Molly just shook her head in despair and clutched at Rae's hands. "Rae, I'm so sorry! You have to know I would never have said that if I'd known he could hear me. I was just drinking all this wine, and—"

Julian crossed the kitchen in three long steps to where Gabriel still sat at the table, the look on his face unlike anything Rae had ever seen. Gabriel rose cautiously to his feet, shifting uneasily as he turned to face Julian.

"Which side did Cromfield break, again?" Julian asked softly. There was a quiet anger simmering behind the words that sent chills down Rae's spine.

Gabriel glanced down automatically, taking a nervous step back. Before he could even look up again, Julian punched him with devastating strength right in the ribs. There was a sickening crunch as old wounds broke open, and Gabriel doubled over onto the table with a silent cry of pain.

"JULES!" Angel shouted, shoving him aside so she could examine her brother.

Julian was staring down with complete indifference, watching Gabriel bleed through his shirt and onto the table. As Angel knelt down beside him, gently lifting the fabric so she could get a better look at what was going on, Julian's eyes lifted and locked onto Rae's.

It was as though he'd punched her too. She flinched at the disappointment and righteous anger there, wishing he had used his fists instead. It would have hurt less.

HOW DID I LET THIS HAPPEN?!

"Go," he commanded, so quiet that only she could hear, "go fix this. NOW!"

It was as if she'd unfrozen. All at once a flood of blood and adrenaline rushed back through her limbs, and she pulled herself up from the table in one smooth movement. She was out the door the next second, hearing the aftermath of her little disaster as she headed for the stairs.

"Julian, you get away from him!" Angel was yelling. "Don't make me freeze you!"

Thank goodness they owned the entire top floor and didn't have any neighbors. Or, if they did, Rae didn't know any of them.

Still, at this rate perhaps it would be wise to purchase the floor below as well.

Although they were living countless levels up, Rae knew it would still be quicker for her to take the stairs than the elevator. She switched into Jennifer's leopard and flew down story after story at a speed so fast she knew even the security cameras couldn't detect it.

If she could just make it to the park, she thought there was a chance she could still catch him before he made it home to his car. At that point there was no telling where he might go.

He would be too responsible to use his tatù out in the open, no matter how he was feeling, and therein laid her only possible advantage. *She* was not so responsible, and would risk that and more to get him back. Then again, judging by the look on his face before he left, maybe he wasn't feeling all that responsible either...

Her eyes filled with burning, guilty tears as the image flashed through her mind: Devon standing with his hand frozen in the air, a look of complete surprise paling his handsome face.

"You and Gabriel?"

She'd never seen him look so lost, so betrayed, so hurt all at once. Not since his father had thrown him out of Guilder and disowned him—and even then—it wasn't as bad as this.

A shudder ran through her body as she recalled the second half of that image.

As devastated as he'd looked when he first heard, just a split second later he was completely unreachable to her. Walled up and cold. Indifferent and numb. He'd removed himself to a place she couldn't follow. Safe-guarding what was left of his feelings.

And no matter what she did, or what ended up happening, she had a sinking feeling that unless she got to him soon there was a chance he could be lost to her forever.

She pushed herself even harder, leaping down the remaining five stories and throwing her body against the door to the lobby. It was here that she came to an infuriating pause, smoothing down her hair and walking slowly past Raphael, the long-suffering lobby attendant, as she made her way to the front door.

"Evening, Raph," she said politely, trying to catch her breath.

"Evening, Miss Kerrigan," he said, delighted to have someone to converse with. "Hey," he got excitedly to his feet, "you didn't happen to catch that last episode of—"

"Sorry, Raph," she held up her hand and speed-walked to the door, "can't talk!"

She pushed open the door and raced out onto the sidewalk. The frigid night air bit into her skin, scantily-covered by her hastily conjured dress. On any other day she would have conjured herself a thick jacket, but tonight there was no time.

After glancing around quickly to make sure that no one remained the wiser, she switched once more into Jennifer's ink and took off, darting this way and that between the trees.

I'll just explain everything, she thought as she ran. *I'll just be perfectly honest and explain everything from the very beginning. After all, nothing even happened!*

But for the first time ever another little voice popped up in the back of her head, splintered off from the first. A soft but determined voice of dissent.

...nothing even happened—besides that kiss.

I can explain the kiss too. I was in shock. I didn't realize what was happening until—

...until you kissed him back?

I didn't MEAN to kiss him back. I just...it just happened!

...but you'd thought about doing it before. A part of you wanted to—

Shut up! That's not true!

One hand flew up to her head as if to knock the warring side loose.

...you know it's true. There's no law that says you can't love two people at the same time—

I'm in LOVE with Devon. I WANT Devon!

...but you want Gabriel too.

WHOSE SIDE ARE YOU ON, ANYWAY?!

The ground flew out from under her feet as she knocked into something hard.

"Ouch," she gasped, blinking to recover herself as two arms held her straight. Then her face paled in horror. At that speed, she could have seriously hurt whoever she barreled into. She looked up in a fright. "I'm so sorry, I wasn't—"

It was Devon.

He was holding her steady, looking down without a hint of emotion or reprieve. The second she was standing straight, he let her go, taking a step away.

"You shouldn't use your tatù out in public. You know better."

Rae panted softly, still trying to catch her breath. The two voices in her head were dead-quiet now—both waiting to see what would happen next.

"I know. I just...had to find you."

He put his hands in his pockets, still staring down at her with that cool indifference she didn't quite know what to make of. "You found me."

Ball in your court, Rae.

"Uh...right."

She glanced down at her feet, searching for the magical words that would make this all better, that would make this all just go away. But as she stared back up into his eyes, his lovely, guarded eyes, she came up blank.

Finally, he shifted impatiently and glanced over her head at the darkened trees. "Let me help you. 'I hooked up with Gabriel, Devon. It's over between us."

"But I didn't hook up with Gabriel," she whispered, struggling to breathe against a sudden heavy weight pressing down on her heart. "And it's not...it can't be over between us..."

For the first time, Devon showed a hint of life. Just a hint.

"You didn't hook up with him?"

Rae took a shaky breath and pulled herself together, determined to get everything out in the open, no matter how painful it might be. "Victor Mallins showed up right after you left yesterday morning. He took me out to lunch and basically said that no matter what the Privy Council might have voted, both he and I still knew I was a walking, talking, ticking time-bomb. A constant threat to everyone around me. When I got back, I kind of had a meltdown. Gabriel was there, and he...he took care of me. That's it. He talked it out with me while I cried." Her eyes flickered up to see how Devon was taking all of this, but he gave absolutely nothing away.

He just stared at her with that same poker-face.

"We were in Molly's room because I shocked him halfway across the apartment. And we weren't naked, we were in towels. He'd been taking a shower, and I'd slipped in my dessert and got it all over me so I had to change." Even as she said it out loud she realized how stupid it must sound.

Devon seemed to think so too. He was quiet for a long time before he finally asked, "Why did you shock him halfway across the apartment?"

She braced herself, every inch of her dreading what was coming next.

"Because he kissed me."

Devon's eyes flickered up and he looked her hard in the eyes—as hard as he ever had.

"*He* kissed you?"

A little shiver ran through her body as she placed her final card on the table. "We... kissed."

His mask slipped for just a split second and she saw his heart shatter a million times behind his careful eyes. Without stopping to think, she reached for him.

"Devon, I—"

For possibly the first time ever, he pulled away, like her touch burned him. He moved backwards a few steps, gathering himself together, before doing the scariest thing of all.

He laughed. "Of course you did."

Rae froze where she stood, one hand still reaching for him. "What do...what does that mean?" She was almost too frightened to ask, but had to.

"A guy shows up, working for the man who's ruining our lives, undermining everything we're working so hard to save. He wants to kill you, only deciding at the last minute to spare your life. He insults your friends, insults your boyfriend, insults you by not respecting what you *said* you wanted..."

What you *said* you wanted. The emphasis was not lost on Rae.

The corners of Devon's lips turned up in a hard, almost manic smile. "...so of course, you, Rae Kerrigan, do the only thing that makes sense. You kiss him."

In all her life Devon had never said her name like that. Never said it in the way that every other person she had ever met had slipped into at one point or another. He'd always held them separate, her and her name. Never blamed one on the other. Until today.

But she couldn't have done anything more to deserve it.

A rush of tears slipped down her cheeks and she slowly lowered her hand. "Devon, I'm so sorry." It was little more than a whisper, but after tonight they both knew he could still hear it.

It had no effect on him, though. He simply stood there, lost in his own thoughts as the smile slowly faded off his face. "I don't know why..." He ran his hands back through his hair with a sigh, "I don't know why I thought anything would be different."

Rae lurched forward, latching onto anything and everything she could. "I'm sorry; you didn't know how—"

"This was exactly the talk we had before we left Scotland. The talk where I said we needed space and you swore to me it had nothing to do with Gabriel." Upon saying the name, his face clouded again before he willfully forced it to be clear. "I don't know why I thought that anything would be different now that we're back in London."

"Devon, that day in Scotland, when I was headed back downstairs—I turned around," Rae muttered quickly but quietly, praying for him to believe her and understand. "I realized what a huge mistake it was for us to take a step apart, instead of moving forward together, and I turned around. I was racing to your room to tell you that. That's how I found you so fast after Kraigan..."

"And what were you going to tell me, exactly?" Devon asked, closing the space between them as he stared down at her. "That you were absolutely sure of where you and I stood? That you were one hundred percent ready to dive into this second chance we'd been given?" His eyes narrowed almost imperceptibly. "That this had nothing to do with Gabriel?"

Rae sobbed once before catching herself, her shoulders buckling as her face fell. "Yes, that's exactly what I was going to tell you."

Devon sighed again, reaching out in spite of himself to wipe a tear from her cheek. "Why did you kiss him?"

I didn't know what I was doing. It happened before I could stop myself. I'd never do it again in a million—

"Because a part of me wanted to," she whispered. "I saw how he felt about me, when I used Carter's tatù. I...I saw how he felt. And I don't feel that way about him, but...I think a part of me wanted to."

Devon's jaw tightened and he dropped his hand. "Because he isn't me?"

"Because there isn't anything to him."

The second Rae said the words, she realized they were true. That magical phrase that had been escaping her—the simple explanation to explain her nightmarishly jumbled feelings as of late—that's exactly what it was.

Devon shook his head. "I don't know what that means."

"He *isn't* you, Devon," Rae said softly, trying her best to explain. "He isn't humble and kind. He isn't dependable and sure. He hasn't seen me through the darkest moments of my life, so when he looks at me...the weight of that isn't there behind his eyes." She reached again for his hands, and this time he allowed her to take them. "He doesn't love me unconditionally, Devon. And I don't love him that way. He's just simple, easy, unpredictable." The last word slipped out before she could stop it. "Free."

Devon's hands stiffened. "And that's what you want? To be free?"

She shook her head wildly from side to side. "No! I want to be with you! I want to be with you *forever*—through *everything*! No matter what it takes, I want to carve out a future with you and make everything trying to stop that from happening fall on its knees and watch." She took a step closer to him, tilting her face up to his. "I want *you*, Devon. I always have, I always will."

For a moment he looked tempted. In fact, he looked so lured that for a split second he actually started leaning down.

But then his eyes tightened and he pulled away.

"But I can't believe you. I can't trust you."

The weight that had been slowly crushing her heart finished the job.

She blinked, suddenly chilled in the rush of cool air that filled the space between them.

"What? Of course you—"

"Rae, I can't be those things for you," he said matter-of-factly. "I can't love you less. I can't un-see what I've seen. I can't erase the weight of the history we have between us." He shook his head sadly, gazing at her like there was nothing more in the world he wanted to do than lift her up into his arms, but a weight of his own wasn't letting him. "I think that's what makes us so strong. This isn't something light and meaningless than can blow away at the first sign of trouble. This isn't something uncertain. You can count on this. You can trust it. I'd trust it with my life." He took a step back, still shaking his head. "But if you feel like it's a weight holding you back..."

"Devon," Rae blurted, seeing the sudden direction this was taking, "*please* don't leave. I can't...I can't believe this is happening right now." She sank into a crouch and ran her fingers back through her hair, muttering almost to herself, "How did I let this happen?"

He paused at the end of the clearing, watching her fall apart.

"I am so, *so* sorry," she wept. "I never meant to hurt you—I would never do *anything* to hurt you. I want you with all my heart, I'm just trying to be—" Her throat choked up as she sobbed once more. "Devon, I'm so sorry I kissed him!"

"Hey..."

A pair of strong arms lifted her to her feet once more. He held her until she was finally able to stop crying. Not cradled against himself like he usually would, just secure and strong.

She realized with a shudder it was the way he would hold a friend.

"It's not that you kissed him," he murmured. She looked up in alarm, and he was quick to clarify. "Don't get me wrong, I can't believe you—" He took a deep breath and tried to steady himself. "It's how you felt when you did. It wasn't some accident, some passing attraction. Truth be told, I'm not even sure it was Gabriel himself. There's something about *us* you're not sure about. And that...I can't help you with. That's something you have to figure out on your own."

"Devon," she grasped fistfuls of his coat, refusing to let him pull away, "I am absolutely sure about you. I'm sure that—"

"But you're not sure about *us*," he said softly. "Be honest with yourself, Rae."

She fell silent. The problem with Devon was that before he was her boyfriend he was her friend. He knew her well. Sometimes even better than she knew herself.

"I can't stop loving you," he continued in that same, gentle voice. "You're it for me. That's never going to change. But right now...I think you need some time. To sort things through."

She shook her head, feeling like she was melting away from the inside out. "I don't want that."

"But you need to."

"So that's it?" The words caught in her throat as she lifted her eyes to his, unwilling to believe they could be true. "You're breaking up with me?"

"No, Rae." He flashed a sad smile before disappearing into the night. "You broke up with me."

Chapter 14

Rae didn't remember the walk back through the park that night. She had no idea how she got home. From the minute she and Devon parted ways, each heading in a separate direction, it was as if she went into some sort of fugue state—completely unaware of the world around her. Like when she had found out she was immortal.

She vaguely remembered pushing open the doors to the lobby. It was late, after one in the morning, but that didn't stop loyal Raphael from leaping to his feet the second he saw her.

"Miss Kerrigan!" he cried, rushing forward. "I'm so glad I caught you. I was trying to tell you earlier but—"

"Not now, Raph," she kept one foot moving in front of the other, eyes locked on the elevator at the end of the hall. "We'll talk in the morning, okay?"

"But Miss Kerrigan—"

"Raph, it's not a good—"

"Your boyfriend wanted me to give you this!" He waved his arm between them and it was only then that Rae realized he was holding something in his hands.

It was a key. A little silver key with no note or explanation.

Rae's heart skipped a beat as she picked it up with trembling fingers. She'd only given a key to one other person.

"Mr. Wardell left it for you at the front desk when he left earlier this evening," Raphael said a little nervously, eyeing Rae's face with obvious concern. "He said you'd know why."

So that was it, huh? Devon had known what was going to happen before she even met up with him in the park. Before they'd even ended things officially, he had known it was over.

She slipped it into her pocket but was temporarily unable to speak. Her mouth went dry and she tried to swallow. It took more effort than it should. Shoot, breathing took more effort as well.

"You and Miss Skye sure get a lot of foot-traffic going in and out of your place," Raphael joked good-naturedly, trying to lighten the mood.

"Yeah, well," Rae's voice came out scratchy and low, "it looks like there's going to be one less person for you to worry about. 'Night Raphael." Without another word she headed for the elevator and pushed the button to go to the top floor. The second the double doors were closed, she collapsed against them, bringing her hands up over her face and doubling over in a silent scream.

How could this have happened?

She and Devon started out the morning in bed, wrapped up together in a tangle of sheets and limbs, and complete and utter bliss.

Now...?

The elevator dinged, and she stepped slowly through the doors into the penthouse. It was empty. The peace and quiet she'd been searching for since yesterday morning was finally here.

Great.

A parade of hot tears streamed down her face as she stood in the doorway, shivering.

That's just great.

Just to be sure she was alone she went from room to room, checking for inhabitants. No one was there. She assumed that Luke and Molly had gone back to his place, and Julian and Angel had gone back to his. As for Gabriel...Rae found she didn't much care where he was.

Once she was done making her sweep, she headed off to take a long shower—only to pull immediately back when she saw her pile of wet, dessert-stained clothes on the tile floor. She stared at them for a moment, still silently crying, before she left to take a shower in Molly's bathroom instead. When she was finished, she conjured herself some thick pajamas and padded her way across the quiet living room to climb into bed.

The sheets were freezing with no one else there to heat them, and she curled into a little ball, holding her knees to her chest as the sadness washed over her in heartbreaking waves. She wanted her Mom. She wanted Uncle Argyle and Aunt Linda. She wanted to go home. Except she didn't know where home was. Everything sucked.

I deserve this, she thought with self-loathing as she lay there by herself. *If anyone deserves this, it has to be me.*

Ever since Devon had come into her life all those years ago, he had been perfect. She said that with no exaggeration, bias, or pretense. Ask anyone and they would tell you the same thing.

Devon was perfect. The perfect gentleman, the perfect agent, the perfect friend, boyfriend, lover. There was not a single thing he couldn't, and wouldn't, do for the people he loved.

When she needed a mentor, he taught her the ropes. When she needed a friend, he stood by her against the world. When she needed a rescue, he jumped off a cliff. When she needed to live, his body found a way to fly them back up again.

That was Devon.

And what had *she* done?

She'd kissed Gabriel.

Another wave of sobs choked her and she curled herself even tighter, rocking gently back and forth as her tear-damp hair stuck against the pillow.

How could she be so stupid? How could she risk something as precious as him? When he was the *one kind thing* life had seen fit to throw her way...

But even as she thought the words, a sudden surge of anger mixed in with the sadness like a poisonous drug. It wound its way through her otherwise-despairing brain, corrupting everything it touched like a cancer.

She might have ruined her life tonight. But she certainly hadn't done it alone. She'd had help.

The persistent, unrelenting, refused-to-wear-a-shirt kind of help...

Ten minutes later Rae was pounding on Gabriel's door. She'd used Julian's ability to find him. The hotel where he was staying wasn't far from the penthouse, and although she was too respectful of Devon's warning to use her tatù again in public, it had taken almost no effort to con Raphael out of his car keys.

"I'm coming, I'm coming," she heard Gabriel grumble from the other side of the door.

It was coming up on three in the morning, and by now most everyone on the hotel floor was asleep. There was a soft shuffling sound, and then the door opened to reveal a recently awoken Gabriel, squinting at her with bloodshot eyes.

Eyes that widened slightly when they took in her general appearance. She hadn't bothered to change out of the flannel pajama set she'd conjured. His gaze came to rest on her face.

"Rae, are you..." he winced slightly as he pulled open the door, "are you okay?"

She didn't say a word; she just pushed past him and stormed into his room.

It was untidy, like she would have guessed, with clothes and random receipts and other bits of mess strewn out all over the floor. There was a little nest of sheets in the middle of the bed from where he'd been sleeping, and a pile of bloody bandages lay in the trash.

The blood threw her for a minute and she just stood there. "Julian really got you good, didn't he?"

"You know...I always discount the psychic." Gabriel winced again as he shut the door and flipped on a light. "Dumb mistake."

He was wearing a pair of boxers and a loose black tank, presumably to give his newly injured ribs as much room as possible. His blond hair was as shaggy as ever and still faintly damp from his nightly shower, filling the air between them with that same mouthwatering citrus smell.

"Devon broke up with me," she said with no further preamble. Her voice was choppy. Clipped. And very, very angry. No matter how many deep breaths she'd taken to steady herself on the way here, there was only a very thin layer of control keeping her from crossing the room and ripping Gabriel's beautiful head off. As partially misdirected as that might be, she believed deep down that it would make her feel better.

Gabriel's eyebrows shot up in genuine surprise. "He did?" Words failed him and he shook his head. "*Wow*," he said softly. "I didn't think he'd ever do that."

Rae folded her arms tightly across her chest and glared. "Yeah, me neither."

It was only then that Gabriel seemed to realize she was angry with him. Again, his face lit in mild surprise before he folded his own arms defensively across his chest. "So I'm guessing you came here for sex then?"

An alarm clock shattered in a million pieces against the door above his head.

"...I'll take that as a no."

"How could you do this?!" she screamed, letting out all her anger at once.

Oh yes, their kiss included two people, she was well aware of that. But Gabriel's sabotage had started long before that, and after the day she'd had she was either unwilling or unable to cry for even another second. She needed to yell instead. And while she might deserve a good yelling at herself, Gabriel certainly had earned one as well.

"Me?!" he exclaimed. "I'm not the one who broke up with you, Rae. And I'm not the one who went around kissing someone else when they had a boyfriend."

A coffee pot shattered on the remains of the clock.

"Hey," he yelled, ducking down to avoid the shards, "you're going to have to pay for that!"

"It's your fault!"

"I didn't do anything!"

"You didn't do *anything*?!" she screamed back, beyond all reason. "*Really?!*"

"Okay, fine," he conceded, "so I'm constantly trying to get into your pants—"

"*You caught my arm, Gabriel!*"

The room fell suddenly quiet between them. The only movement was the rapid rise and fall of Rae's chest as her body literally vibrated with pent-up rage.

"You saved my life! You didn't let me fall!" She fired out each one as an accusation, eyes flashing blue fire as she concluded. "*You fell in love with me!*"

This time it was *his* face that darkened in a wild rage.

"I knew it! I knew you used Carter's tatù on me! Who the *hell* do you think you—"

"Of course I used it on you!" Rae realized she was standing on her toes, almost levitating off the ground she was so beside herself. "You were going to kill me and then you switched sides. I had to know what made you do that. I had to make sure it was safe for the rest of them—"

"Oh, don't give me that *bullshit!*" he cut her off, storming across the room to face her. "You *wanted* to know. That's why you did it. And you're not sorry you did."

"No," her voice was quieter now, and trembling, "I am sorry I did. I wish I had never seen what I did. I wish I didn't—" She fought back a sob, and turned for the door. "I should never have even come here."

But before she had taken two steps he grabbed her by the arms, spinning her back around to face him. "No, you don't get to just leave. You don't get to storm in here, say what you said, and just go."

"Let go of me—"

But he just held on tighter, keeping his long fingers wrapped around her arms as he leaned down and stared right into her eyes. "So Devon broke up with you..." His eyes dilated with intensity, scanning her face for every detail. "What does that mean for us?"

Her mouth fell open in shock. "For...*us*?"

He nodded swiftly, tightening his fingers in a little squeeze. "Yeah, us."

The walls seemed to close in around her as she wrenched herself free and took a step back. "I come here and tell you that the love of my life just left me in a park in the middle of the night, and the first thing you want to know is...when do you and I jump into the sack?"

His face flushed slightly and he bowed his head. "Rae, that's not what I meant. I'm sure this night's been really hard on you; I just—"

She held up a hand and shook her head, seeing him in a whole new light.

"I found a man I loved, who loved me. Who I wanted to have a future with. Who I was willing to risk everything for. Why on earth would you think...?"

"Why on earth would I think...what?" He looked a little offended now, but he kept his temper under control and his voice as steady as hers. "You fell in love with someone *you* want a future with? Who *you* were willing to risk everything for?" He threw his hands in the air and shook his head. "There's an attraction here, Rae. There has been from the second we met. You can't deny—"

"—that it's an *attraction*?" she interrupted. "Yeah, Gabriel. I'm attracted. But there's such a huge difference between that and..." Her voice trailed off and she looked him squarely in the eyes. "Gabriel, there is no *us*."

As soon as she said it she knew it was true.

"There never will be an 'us'." She had come here expecting to fight, expecting to throw things and yell it out. Expecting to try to make him feel at least a little bit as bad as she was feeling herself.

What she didn't expect was that she was going to come here and close a door forever.

But that's exactly what she had done.

In the course of one never-ending day, Rae had kissed two men, loved two men—albeit in very different ways—said goodbye to two men...and eaten a rabbit. She couldn't help but tag that one on the end, no matter how much it didn't relate to her problems at present. The entire world had turned upside down in the course of just twenty-four hours.

So when she opened her eyes to a stream of bright sunlight pouring into her room the next morning, it was more than understandable that she'd be a little hesitant to get out of bed.

Who knew what tragedy awaited her today?

As if to answer her question, there was a soft knock on her bedroom window.

At first she looked around in confusion. Then her heart leapt into her throat as she bolted upright with a beaming smile. *Outside* her bedroom window? Up on the *fifth* story? That could only mean—"

"Thank the Maker!" she whispered to herself, throwing on a silk bathrobe as she hurried to unlock it. She pulled back the curtains in the same movement, wincing slightly as the bright morning sun shot into her eyes. "Devon, I—"

But it wasn't Devon. In fact, it was one of the last people she expected to see hanging like a monkey from the roof outside her window.

"Let me in, Kerrigan." Angel lifted one hand off the ledge above her and frowned at the scuff marks on her glove. "Damn! This is Chanel."

Rae blinked.

Then Angel literally kicked her aside and she remembered she was supposed to move.

"What the hell are you doing here?" she demanded, peering down over the ledge to make sure no one had seen her early-morning visitor. "Why didn't you use the elevator?"

Angel landed gracefully beside the bed, brushing herself off and placing her gloves neatly in her jacket pocket. "I didn't have a key," she explained lightly, indifferent to the absurd strangeness of the feat she'd just performed. "And I didn't want your roommate or anyone else to know I came here."

"Molly's gone," Rae said shortly as she pulled the window closed. "So is everyone else. I don't think...I don't think they wanted to be around when I got back."

Angel looked at her shrewdly, and for a split second Rae was almost glad that the first person she was seeing upon 'emotional re-entry' was Julian's odd girlfriend. Out of everyone here, Angel had the least stake in whatever had happened last night. She was a girl who spoke her mind and wouldn't hesitate to tell Rae nothing but the honest truth.

"You made a giant freaking mess yesterday, you little monster. You should be ashamed."

Honestly was overrated.

Rae glared and snatched up her robe belt, feeling like a mess of tattered emotions and raw nerves. Maybe Angel wasn't the best person for her to be seeing right now after all. "Good morning to you too," she muttered, tying the belt.

Angel was unamused. "I went and saw Gabriel last night. He's a mess. Said he'd made a giant mistake in sticking around here, and that if he and I knew what was best for us we would cut our losses and just go."

Despite her early morning fatigue, Rae was stunned. Her mouth fell open as the familiar sting of coming tears pricked at the corner of her eyes. "He said that?" she asked quietly.

"Yeah, he did."

Angel paced angrily back and forth, either oblivious or just completely indifferent to the effect her words were having. Not that Rae was surprised. She had a feeling it would take a lot to make Angel really care about something. With her white-blond hair and sleek black leather jumpsuit, she reminded Rae a bit of a young Jennifer Jones. A literal angel with a giant chip on her shoulder.

She must have truly fallen head over heels for Julian to have let him get so close.

"Not that it matters," she continued. "After what you and Gabriel did, Julian isn't going to allow him to set foot in this house."

Rae remembered the look on Julian's face right before he hit Gabriel, and she sank down onto her bed with a shaky sigh. She had been so caught up in how this mess was destroying the three of them—her, Devon, and Gabriel—that she hadn't had time yet to think about how it was affecting everyone else. They were a tight-knit group, the lot of them. It would take quite a bit to get in between them, and now that something had she wasn't quite sure what to do about it. She'd messed it all up. Things would never be the same again.

A quick tapping caught Rae's attention, and she looked up to see Angel bouncing her foot impatiently against the floor with her arms folded tightly over her chest. "So?"

"So, what?" Rae shot back, on the verge of tears but determined not to show it.

Angel's icy blue eyes narrowed. "*So,* I didn't come all this way, survive everything I've survived, just to have to choose between my brother and my boyfriend. You need to fix this."

And with those five words it was like something in Rae finally just snapped.

Cromfield and Mallins? Devon and Gabriel? And her at the center of it all?

It was all just too much.

"*Really?*" she demanded, uncontrollable tears finally spilling over. "*That's* what you came all the way here to tell me? That I need to fix this?" Her voice shook as it rose in panic. "Like I don't know that already? Like my *entire life* isn't already falling apart?!"

Without another word, she physically and emotionally crumbled into Angel's unsuspecting arms, sobbing without restraint onto her hard, leather-clad shoulder. She didn't mean to. She certainly wasn't planning to. But there was only so much emotional turmoil one girl could take.

"Whoa, there." Angel caught her stiffly, freezing for a moment before lowering her hands uncertainly to pat her on the back. "Uh...you know I don't do hugs, right?"

Rae just cried harder. Wishing she was anywhere else in the world. Wishing she was laughing with Devon instead of crying with Angel. Wishing Angel was Molly—Molly would have known better than to wear uncomfortable fabrics when there was a chance her friend might cry on them.

"Hey," Angel's voice softened, though she continued discreetly trying to peel Rae away from her, "this is going to be alright. You know boys. Bunch of delicate little flowers. They'll get over it."

Rae shook her head as she finally pulled away. "No. They won't."

Angel sighed and pursed her lips, staring at Rae speculatively. "Do you love Gabriel?"

An image of his face flashed through her head, and Rae hung her head. "No—not in the way he wants me to. Not in the way I love Devon."

"Okay," Angel said briskly, "so Devon it is, then. Problem solved. Stop crying."

"It's not as easy as all that," Rae glared, wiping her face. "He broke up with me."

Angel rolled her eyes. "So make him *un*-break up with you. Honestly, Kerrigan, this is not the Rae who blasted me into that wall in San Francisco. This is not the Rae who threatened to, and I quote, 'cheerfully beat me to death.'"

Rae sank onto the bed in defeat. "What do you want me to do? *Beat* him into taking me back? Try to threaten him into a relationship?"

A flash of mischief shot through Angel's eyes. "Some guys find a little excitement like that to be quite the turn-on."

"Shut up," Rae snorted. "I sincerely doubt Julian would like it if you—"

"*Physicality*, Rae," Angel clarified with a laugh, "not brute force. Honestly, get your mind out of the gutter."

Rae pushed back her curls with a shaky smile and tried to gather herself together. Not the easiest task. Her face was swollen from crying so hard the night before, and as she felt around in her hair she realized there were still leaves from the park and a little shard of plastic from the alarm clock buried inside.

Perfect. A testament to my misery and shame. I'm like a piece of walking, talking performance art.

"Yeah, you look really bad. If that's what you were wondering."

Rae rolled her eyes and pulled her hair back into a ponytail. "Okay, since you're the only one who's here, can you just pretend for a second you weren't raised in a cave by a lunatic and try to show a little human compassion instead?"

Angel leaned back with her hands on her hips. "Okay, first of all—too soon. And second, I know you're freaking out here, okay? I get it. I get it because I know you love Devon as much as I love Julian. And I can't imagine losing Julian."

Rae bit down hard on her lip as another wave of tears slipped down her face. "So, what do you think I should do?"

For the first time, Angel didn't know quite what to say. At first she had been stern and determined, but the longer she stared down at Rae's defeated form, the more her eyes shone with gentle pity. "Well, I *was* going to tell you to get up, stop crying, and pull a 'Rae Kerrigan' to fix all this."

Rae pulled in a ragged breath, keeping her eyes on the floor. "And now?"

"Now...I'm going to tell you to go and fix you."

"What does that mean?"

"I don't know, Rae." Angel frowned sympathetically. "Go get yourself together, find your center. Do what you need to do and go where you need to go. Whatever it is that makes you feel better—do that. 'Cause you're in no state to fix anything right now, and if there's one thing I've learned from Julian it's that you're the glue that holds this group together."

Rae pulled in a shaky breath. "Jules said that?"

"It must be true." Angel shrugged indifferently, but Rae could have sworn she shot her a fleeting smile. "So what's it going to be, Kerrigan? You getting up?"

The tears didn't stop. It seemed there was nothing Rae could do about that. But a sudden force propelled her to her feet as she pulled herself together.

Angel might be a bit crazy but she was right about one thing.

There was someone Rae needed to see...

Chapter 15

"Hi, Mom."

Beth, who had been standing in what used to be the garden, probably taking stock of what was left, whirled around in a cloud of smoke. "Rae?" she asked incredulously, lowering her smoldering hands.

Rae watched her mother's reaction with a faint smile. Not too many other members of the PTA would throw fire from their hands at the first sign of trouble. She could hardly blame her mom for having skittish instincts. Her run-in with Cromfield had taken a toll.

"How many other people call you 'Mom'?" Rae asked cheekily, diverting the point of the question to give herself more time.

In the taxi, in the terminal, in the plane, and then in the other taxi, Rae had been trying her best to figure out what to say. Why was she here? What was so bad it had made her literally *run away to Scotland*? Each time she'd come up blank. And now again.

Blank.

Beth wasn't fooled for an instant. She threw down the rake she'd been holding at once, stomping through the mounds of dirt to take Rae by the hands. "What is it, honey?" she asked, scanning her daughter's eyes. "What's wrong?" When Rae still couldn't say anything, her eyes scanned the driveway behind them. "Is Devon here?"

It was Devon's name that snapped Rae out of it.

The second she heard it she broke down into sudden tears for the millionth time, falling to pieces right there on the front stoop.

"Mom...I've made a terrible mistake."

With the unconditional love of a mother, Beth gathered Rae up in her arms and helped her inside. Once she'd settled her down on the living room sofa, she covered her up with an unnecessary blanket and plied her with hot chocolate and bits of candy until she finally started to come around.

At first Rae had been almost embarrassed. Yes, Beth was her mother, and when a girl went out and lost the love of her life, it was natural to come running home. The thing was that Beth had only technically been her mother for a small amount of time. Rae thought of her as mom, but also thought of her as Beth. It was like she was two different people to her. And just as Beth's instincts were to whirl around with fire, Rae's were most certainly not to go *running home.*

She wouldn't have even considered it if it hadn't been for Angel's unconventional prodding, but the second she had said, 'Whatever it is that makes you feel better—do that,' there was only one face that had popped into her mind. Beth's. Her mom's.

"I'm sorry," she sniffled, smoothing back her hair and trying not to appear as the broken-hearted teenager she most decidedly was. "I didn't mean to just drop in on you like this."

Beth settled herself down on the sofa beside her with a look of surprise. "Drop in on me like this?" she repeated incredulously. "Rae, this is your house. I'm your mother."

Rae shifted uncomfortably. "Yeah, but still. I don't want to just—"

"Honey," Beth interrupted gently, taking her once again by the hands, "what happened?"

The worst thing that could happen, Rae thought to herself. *The worst thing that could ever happen.*

"I kissed Gabriel," she whispered.

Beth closed her eyes and nodded slowly. "Ah. I see."

"And then Devon broke up with me."

This time Beth looked a bit more surprised, but she pressed her lips tight, holding her tongue to let Rae talk.

It was a good thing too, because considering how long Rae had been keeping the rant to herself it suddenly came tumbling out of her.

"And it was a HUGE mistake!" she wailed, sobbing once more. "I don't know what made me do it! I don't know what I was thinking! Ugh! Except that I *do* know what I was thinking, and what I was thinking was all wrong! Of *course* Devon figures us out before I do! He always has to be such a perfect, insufferable, over-achiever. But I can't even make those jokes about him anymore because he...because *I don't have him anymore*!" Her face scrunched up for another long rant as she paused to take her first breath. This must be how Molly felt all the time, this sort of no-oxygen-needed storytelling.

Her mother watched her with sympathetic eyes, which only encouraged Rae to continue her rant.

"And now everything's a mess! Julian broke Gabriel, Gabriel wants to take off with Angel, Molly and Luke vanished, and I don't know if they're mad at me too! And Devon..." She covered her face in her hands and wept. "Mom, nothing matters anymore. It was only him. That was the only thing I ever...and now he's gone." She broke down completely, unable to speak.

Beth gathered her up in her arms, rocking her slowly as she whispered soft words that didn't mean anything specific but helped nonetheless. They stayed that way for a long time, long enough that the short noontime shadows lengthened as the afternoon slowly dragged on. Finally, when Rae was able to catch her breath, she gingerly pulled herself away. Except what she saw almost made her start crying all over again.

"Mom?" she demanded. "You're...*smiling*?!"

"I'm sorry, sweetie!" Beth said quickly, clearing her face into the required, sympathetic frown. But try as she might a hint of a smile kept leaking through. "It's just...and don't take this the wrong way...but a part of me is so happy to hear you say that!"

Rae stiffened angrily and dropped their joined hands. "Don't worry. I won't take that the wrong way."

Beth chuckled. "Oh, honey, that's not what I meant. But you have to understand, when you showed up unannounced at my door, crying like the whole world was about to end...well, with your history there was a legitimate chance that might actually have been about to happen. And when you showed up without any of your friends, looking like someone had torn your heart out, I thought..."

"You thought they were dead."

Beth nodded with a wistful grin. "It's just so...nice that you're actually having some normal teenager problems. As a mother I really couldn't ask for anything more."

Rae shook her head with a reluctant grin of her own.

How completely and utterly bizarre her life had become.

She flashed back for a random moment to the girl on the train, a younger version of Rae, racing through the city and across the rolling green hills to see the gates of Guilder for the first time. The girl who marveled out her window at an eagle that was flying with them so close, not knowing at the time that the eagle was actually a boy with whom she would soon share a study group.

How would *that* girl have reacted to *this* day?

Would she have been ashamed with the way Rae had handled things? Would she have fallen just as easily into the same common pitfalls of teenage romance? Would she have believed on any level that she would be sitting here, having this conversation with her *mother*?

But even then, as Rae was soaking in the nostalgia, another thought came to mind. A rather obvious one she was surprised she hadn't considered before.

Follow that same girl just an hour later. She'd just met Molly, she was walking out of Aumbry House—her new home—when a scream from the construction men working above caught her attention. She looked up to see a plank falling in slow motion towards her. Yes, even on her very first day at Guilder, she'd been about to die.

Then she was in his arms.

Devon Wardell.

The boy who would go on to become her mentor. The boy she would continue to pine after for the next year of her life. The boy who, unfortunately at the time, had another girlfriend.

And in that moment it was as clear to her as it had ever been. The answer she'd been searching for. The intangible reassurance that she was doing the right thing.

Rae had fallen in love with Devon that very day.

That girl had fallen in love with *that* boy. Before there were masked villains. Before there were sinister agendas and hidden plots. Before any of that—they had loved each other.

There was no weight to it. It was the simplest thing in the world. As easy as breathing.

Devon Wardell was her one true love.

Just thinking the words brought a radiant smile to her face.

And she was going to get him back.

"Mom, I need to use your phone..."

There was just one problem with Rae's brilliant phone idea, no matter how flushed with sudden illumination she might be: She and her mom were still in the middle of rural Scotland.

"But how do you live like this?" she demanded, pacing around the kitchen in little circles as she waved her phone above her head. "I mean, what if I had some kind of emergency? How would people even reach you? What would you have done?"

Beth rolled her eyes, leaning back against the counter with a look of strained patience. She had been watching this little dance for a good long while now. "To be honest, honey, if *you* had some kind of emergency, I'm sure I would hear about it on the morning news."

"Very funny," Rae shot back, still holding the phone above her head as she searched for a signal. "*Wait a minute*! I think I have a..." Her face fell. "Nope. False alarm."

Beth sighed in exasperation. "Just call him on the landline."

"I told you, I don't have his number."

"Rae Kerrigan," Beth folded her arms across her chest, "how the hell could you possibly not know your own boyfriend's phone number?"

Rae bristled defensively. "It's a generational thing, Mom. Why would I ever *need* to know it? It was in my *phone*. That's the whole point of a phone."

"Looks like it's not a very good point then, huh?"

Rae ignored this. "Well, maybe I should just walk into town—"

"Sweetheart," Beth said coaxingly, prying the phone out of her daughter's hands, "the sun's going down. And despite all your generational know-how, I'm fairly certain you don't know where town is."

Rae was about to make a point about there being GPS on her phone, but she wisely held her tongue.

"More importantly," Beth cautioned, "you told me Devon said he was giving you space, right?"

Rae nodded nervously. "Yeah?"

"Well, no matter what he says I'm sure he needs some space himself. You did break his trust with Gabriel, honey. Now, what's done is done and I understand that, but it sounds like Devon does too. Just trust me; you want to give him a little time."

Rae nodded automatically before her eyes narrowed in suspicion. "Wait a minute, what does that mean? *Trust you*? Did you have some kind of—"

"Let me tell you about another little generation gap, sweetie," Beth began with a cautious smile. "*My* generation doesn't feel the need to share every little detail of their lives like yours does."

Rae crossed her arms over her chest with a grin. "So you're not going to tell me?"

"We also don't post pictures online of our morning toast."

Dinner that night was a rather subdued affair. Rae was too nervous to eat much of anything, too busy planning out exactly what she was going to say to win Devon back. Beth was too nervous watching Rae not eat to eat much of anything herself.

All in all, it was probably one of the quietest family dinners they'd ever had. No one revealed any dark government secrets or spontaneously lit themselves on fire or anything. It was one for the books!

Beth went to bed early that night, having agreed to drive Rae to the airport the next morning, but no matter how long Rae lay atop her queen-sized bed she couldn't seem to close her eyes. There was too much rocketing around in her brain for sleep to even be considered. So at around midnight, moving as quietly as she could so as not to wake her mother, she crept once more out her window and headed down to the barn.

She couldn't tell you exactly what made her decide to go there. Truth be told, the barn had always given her a weird, creepy vibe, and on most days she hated going in there alone.

But tonight was different.

The longer she'd lain in bed, the more she'd thought about it, picturing the tall oak rafters and imagining the smell of hay. Once her feet touched the ground outside the house, they simply started walking towards it as if a force larger than herself was driving her forward.

She pushed open the heavy oak doors and conjured a candle the moment she was inside. A host of long, frightening shadows sprang up from nowhere out of the dark the second the little flame began to flicker. Rae held it bravely out in front of her as she crept silently beneath the high ceilings, reminding herself with every step that, should 'monsters' arise, she had super powers.

When she got to her mother's bench, she paused.

She blamed this bench for a lot, as silly as that might be. It was the very spot where her mother and father had fallen in love, and thus she owed it a rather lot as well.

For the first time, she knelt down to examine it up close, running her fingers up and down the grained wood. There was nothing remarkable about it. Nothing that indicated it was the location of some massive hybrid upheaval that was still rocking the tatùed world today.

With a little sigh she sat herself down in the center, placing the candle beside her as she lowered her head into her hands. What had she expected to find out here anyway? A secret cell phone with magical reception that would allow her to call Devon despite her mother's warnings?

She actually laughed out loud, a quiet sound that echoed back softly in the still night.

Just a bench, Rae. Get a grip and go back inside. You have a boyfriend to reclaim tomorrow.

As she was pushing to her feet, her fingers touched something hard. She looked down in surprise, following the groove as it twirled its way into a pattern.

"What the—?" She grabbed her candle and overturned the little bench with a gasp, staring in wonder at the ornate tree carved into the bottom planks. There was something about the arching shape of it that was familiar. Something about its fragile branches and lethal-looking leaves she had seen before.

She must have stared for a good five minutes before it suddenly clicked.

It was a Japanese Maple. Although the wood carving couldn't depict it properly, she knew that each one of those leaves was a blazing crimson red. It was a shade that made the whole tree look like it had gone up in flames. Her fingers reached out again and traced it gently.

There had been one in her backyard when she was a child. She remembered it because her mother hated the damn thing. It was always dropping leaves in the garden and either she or little Rae would be forced to rake them up. But her father had insisted they keep it. 'An ode to her mother,' he'd always called it. At the time, Rae had thought the whole thing was a big joke—an ode to her mother when her mother despised the tree? But now she saw it differently.

The flaming branches and fire-soaked leaves were a testament to her mother's powerful tatù.

So wait a minute... Rae frowned as she traced the design once more. *If her mother hated the tree, she wouldn't have carved it here. That meant it would have to have been—*

"What were you up to, Mr. Simon Kerrigan?" she murmured softly as she pressed her fingers upon the trunk.

But as she did the strangest thing happened. Her finger sank *into* the trunk.

"Oh shit—"

Before she could call her help, the bench split in half with a loud groan, falling to the ground in two large pieces that rolled to the side.

As fast as it had all happened, it was over, and Rae lay there on the ground, blinking in amazement and trying to catch her breath.

Yep, that had been her father alright. Only he would have designed the kind of contraption that would have ripped off her fingers if she hadn't yanked them away with a speed tatù.

Her eyes flickered nervously about the barn, worried the sound might have woken her mother. But the barn and the house were both quiet as a grave, fast asleep on the warm summer night. Then she glanced back at the broken pieces of what was once her mother's prized bench.

That's just wonderful, she thought with a groan. *First I make her drive me to the airport at six in the morning, and then I break her 'seven minutes in heaven with Simon' bench.*

She crawled forward on her hands and knees to examine the damage, wondering if there was a way she could fix it. For the first time in quite a while, there was a warm hum under her skin as Nic MacGyver's tatù floated to the surface. Nic was Guilder's resident handyman-slash-genius. Rae had always thought it was hilarious that he'd been named after his fictional counterpart on television, but upon voicing that to her other Guilder peers it was quickly apparent none of them had any idea what she was talking about. Apparently their Nic MacGyver was the one and only.

A dozen random ideas about homemade wood glue and bolts for leverage flashed through her mind, but before she had a chance to focus on any of them a sliver of white paper caught her eye instead. It was nestled inside one of the halves of the bench, which she just now realized was hollow. Inching forward to get a better look, she reached inside to pull out an oversized white envelope, slightly yellowed around the edges and dampened by rain.

She turned it over slowly, bracing herself for whatever was to come, before her mouth fell open with a loud gasp.

There, written in the center in a fancy script, were two single words:

Rae Kerrigan.

"Honey, are you sure you don't want me to go with you back to London?" Beth asked as she helped unload an overnight bag Rae had conjured from the car. "I could help you settle into your new place? Keep your warring boys at bay?"

"Ha, ha," Rae said sarcastically, but she turned with a grin. "That's really nice of you, but...no thanks. I think this is probably something I should be doing on my own."

Beth pursed her lips but nodded, pulling Rae in for a huge hug. "Alright, well you just have a safe flight and call me as soon as you land, okay? And don't let Molly boss you around about designing the apartment. It's your home too, you hear me?"

Rae chuckled. "Could *you* make that promise? With *Molly*?"

"No, probably not." Beth laughed and hugged her quickly again, before glancing nervously to where she'd illegally double-parked against the curb. "I'd better go. But we'll see each other soon, alright? And remember to call me right when you land!"

"I will!" Rae smiled and waved, watching as her mother smiled sweetly at the parking attendant before slipping behind the wheel of her Lexus and shooting off down the road.

In truth, she would have loved her mother to go with her back to London. It would have been kind of nice to have a shield between her and her angry friends. Not to mention, if anyone could talk Molly down about the apartment—not that something like that would ever realistically happen—it would be Beth. But there was one little problem standing in the way.

Rae wasn't going to London.

The second her mother was out of sight, she headed away from the terminal and doubled back towards the rental car agency. After conjuring herself a Scottish driver's license of the proper age, she was speeding down the interstate heading north, her father's letter safe in her pocket.

About three hours later, she rolled to a stop in a little town on the Dunnett Head Peninsula—a lovely realm of high cliffs and emerald green meadows at the northern tip of Scotland.

She shivered as she stepped out of the car and quickly ducked back in to conjure herself a proper jacket. It was much colder here than even her mother's house, although they weren't too terribly far away. That was most likely because the entire town stood upon fifty-foot cliffs that dropped straight down into a crashing sea.

As Rae pulled her new coat tighter up around her chin, she couldn't help but smile as a misty ocean breeze blew her dark hair up around her. There was something almost magical about this place, she decided as she looked around. It was the kind of place you'd see when you opened the pages of a fairytale, all deep greens and dark blues. Complete with a sparkling ocean, stretching as far as the eye could see.

Then Rae remembered why she was here and her grin faded. She was here because her father had come here. He hadn't said so in his letter, but the letter wasn't the only thing inside the envelope. There was also a key.

Normally she would have been incensed by the trail of cryptic clues, but in this case there was nothing cryptic about it at all. The key was labeled quite clearly: 'Dunnett Head Inn, Bed and Breakfast.' So here she was, key in hand, ready for whatever dear old dad had to throw at her.

A quick drive through the town revealed that the Dunnett Head Inn was actually the only place to stay in the whole tiny city. She caused quite a stir as she checked herself into the correct room—her key had said #4—and settled in. Apparently the local townsfolk didn't get many visitors all the way up here, and when a young girl drove up by herself it caused quite the stir indeed.

Once she was safely inside she once again unfurled the letter, taking in her father's script with almost hungry eyes.

My dearest daughter,

Rae, if you're reading this, then you have grown up to become everything I'd hoped you'd be. You are resourceful and strong, but most importantly you are curious. If there's one thing I can impart to you, sweet daughter, it's that curiosity is the most important gift of them all. The desire to ask questions, to challenge what one has been taught. It is an invaluable lesson, and one I hope you learn as I did.

But I digress. Rae, I'm writing to you, assumedly from the grave, to warn you of the dangers in the world you have entered. Be cautious, think carefully, and ask questions before aligning yourself with those in power. I promise you, not everything is as it seems.

By now you've no doubt heard terrible things about me. The infamous Simon Kerrigan—they're already saying it. I can only imagine what it must be like to go through life carrying that name. For that, I am sincerely sorry.

But I would challenge that there's also more to being a Kerrigan that meets the eye. More than the members of the Privy Council, and those people back at Guilder would have you believe.

You are SPECIAL, Rae. No matter what anyone tells you. And I am not the only one who thinks so.

Although they may be quick to condemn the work of others, I would ask you to take a closer look at the workings of the high and mighty Privy Council. They were not always as spotless and forthcoming as they would have people think.

You need proof? Ask Peter and Katerina.

You are going to have to dig for answers. Everything you trust and believe in, question it all.

Good luck, Rae. Stay strong and safe. I wish I could be there to guide you through these perilous times, but, alas, that chance has been taken from me. Instead, allow me to impart a few parting words.

The best thing you can do in this world is to know yourself. TRUST YOURSELF. The rest will follow.

Yours in love,

Dad

By now Rae's fingers had worn grooves into the sides of the paper. There were tiny ink smudges in the corner that made her think her father had written this in haste, perhaps looking over his shoulder as he filed it away for safe-keeping. Hoping that one day she would find it. Never knowing for sure if that would be the case.

With careful hands, she folded it back up and pressed it against her heart as she gazed wistfully out the window. She didn't know exactly why she was feeling so sentimental. After all, her father had been a terrible man—the crazed Simon Kerrigan. She knew this. But still... She stroked the back of the paper lovingly. This was the only letter he'd ever give her. The only words of love and advice she would ever remember hearing from her dad.

She didn't know how long she stood there. It must have been a long time. There were no pressing time concerns, because while his letter had certainly brought other issues to light, it had said absolutely nothing as to why he had led her here to Scotland.

The sun began to set low on the horizon over the cliffs, painting the sky in a brilliant orange haze. Eventually, Rae decided to walk out to the bluff to see it for herself.

Yanking a coat and scarf back over her shoulders, she slipped out the side gate to the inn, letter still in hand, and began walking out across the grass towards the ocean. The breeze had picked up stronger than ever, dusting her cheeks in a light layer of ocean salt as walked to the edge of the cliffs.

Gazing out at the horizon, Rae realized she had never seen anything so beautiful. It was as if God Himself had painted this place by hand, streaking the sky and casting handfuls of sparkling glitter down upon the waves. It was so mesmerizing. It was almost painful.

It was then, staring out at the crashing waves that something else caught Rae's attention, a peripheral blaze of color dancing in the corner of her eye. She turned curiously to see that it wasn't a distant fire—like she'd thought—but something stationary. Something she'd seen before. Something that, by now, she almost expected.

A Japanese Maple.

No one was around for miles that far out on the bluffs, so Rae slipped into a tatù and flew across the grass like she had wings, coming to stop in front of the crimson tree. There was nothing about it that lent any sort of hint or idea as to what to do next. The tree itself was the clue.

Rae frowned and circled it slowly. Anything that Simon might have hung or carved or left would have been long worn away by the wind and rain. He would have known that. That meant that everything on the tree itself was out of the question.

So that only left...

Rae closed her eyes and shook her head. A small smile crept up the side of her face, and she actually laughed around as she sank to her knees.

"Okay, Dad, this better be worth it."

Then Rae started to dig.

THE END
Strength & Power
COMING APRIL 2016

~ Turn the page for a teaser of Book 10 ~

Strength & Power

Broken hearted, confused and unsure.

Rae almost feels fifteen years old again... or closer to hundred.

She's hurt the one guy that has sacrificed everything to be with her, the father she believed to be a monster left her a mysterious letter and maybe everything she thought was right might actually be wrong.

A secret clue left by her father sends her on an adventure she might not be prepared to take.

Will she be able to convince Devon she can't life without him?

She has to move fast. Especially when it turns out Devon has a secret of his own...

Sneak Peek

At the Rest of the Series Covers

W.J. May

Strength & POWER

THE CHRONICLES OF KERRIGAN

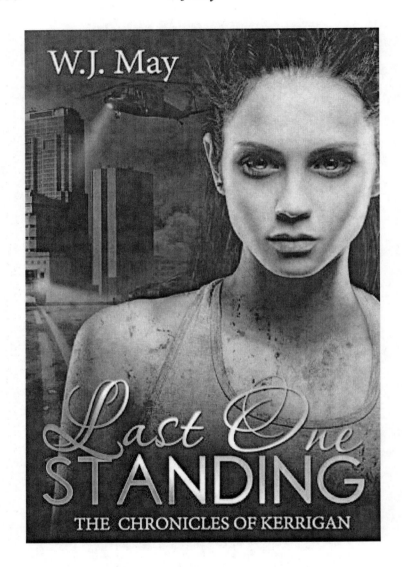

Note from Author

Thanks for reading (and hopefully enjoying Mark of Fate). I feel like we are just starting to know the adult version of Rae, who is still very much her mother, and her father's, child. I love writing about Rae's adventures, her friends and her life! I hope you guys don't mind sticking around for a few more rounds with Rae!

All the best, W.J. May

Newsletter: http://eepurl.com/97aYf

Website: http://www.wanitamay.yolasite.com

Facebook: https://www.facebook.com/pages/Author-WJ-May-FAN-PAGE/141170442608149

The Chronicles of Kerrigan

Book I - *Rae of Hope* **is FREE!**
  Book Trailer:
  http://www.youtube.com/watch?v=gILAwXxx8MU
  Book II - *Dark Nebula*
  Book Trailer:
  http://www.youtube.com/watch?v=Ca24STi_bFM
  Book III - *House of Cards*
  Book IV - *Royal Tea*
  Book V - *Under Fire*
  Book VI - *End in Sight*
  Book VII – *Hidden Darkness*
  Book VIII – *Twisted Together*
  Book IX – *Mark of Fate*
  Book X – *Strength & Power*
  Book XI – *Last One Standing*
  Book XII – *Rae of Light*
  PREQUEL – Christmas Before the Magic

CoK Prequel!

A Novella of the Chronicles of Kerrigan.
A prequel on how Simon Kerrigan met Beth!!
AVAILABLE:

More books by W.J. May

Hidden Secrets Saga:
Download Seventh Mark part 1 For FREE
Book Trailer:
http://www.youtube.com/watch?v=Y-_vVYCIgvo

Like most teenagers, Rouge is trying to figure out who she is and what she wants to be. With little knowledge about her past, she has questions but has never tried to find the answers. Everything changes when she befriends a strangely intoxicating family. Siblings Grace and Michael, appear to have secrets which seem connected to Rouge. Her hunch is confirmed when a horrible incident occurs at an outdoor party. Rouge may be the only one who can find the answer.

An ancient journal, a Sioghra necklace and a special mark force life-altering decisions for a girl who grew up unprepared to fight for her life or others.

All secrets have a cost and Rouge's determination to find the truth can only lead to trouble...or something even more sinister.

RADIUM HALOS - THE SENSELESS SERIES
Book 1 is FREE:

Book Blurb:

Everyone needs to be a hero at one point in their life.

The small town of Elliot Lake will never be the same again.

Caught in a sudden thunderstorm, Zoe, a high school senior from Elliot Lake, and five of her friends take shelter in an abandoned uranium mine. Over the next few days, Zoe's hearing sharpens drastically, beyond what any normal human being can detect. She tells her friends, only to learn that four others have an increased sense as well. Only Kieran, the new boy from Scotland, isn't affected.

Fashioning themselves into superheroes, the group tries to stop the strange occurrences happening in their little town. Muggings, break-ins, disappearances, and murder begin to hit too close to home. It leads the team to think someone knows about their secret - someone who wants them all dead.

An incredulous group of heroes. A traitor in the midst. Some dreams are written in blood.

Courage Runs Red
The Blood Red Series
Book 1 is FREE

What if courage was your only option?

When Kallie lands a college interview with the city's new hot-shot police officer, she has no idea everything in her life is about to change. The detective is young, handsome and seems to have an unnatural ability to stop the increasing local crime rate. Detective Liam's particular interest in Kallie sends her heart and head stumbling over each other.

When a raging blood feud between vampires spills into her home, Kallie gets caught in the middle. Torn between love and family loyalty she must find the courage to fight what she fears the most and possibly risk everything, even if it means dying for those she loves.

Daughter of Darkness
Victoria

Only Death Could Stop Her Now
The Daughters of Darkness is a series of female heroines who
may or may not know each other, but all have the same father,
Vlad Montour.
Victoria is a Hunter Vampire

Free Books:

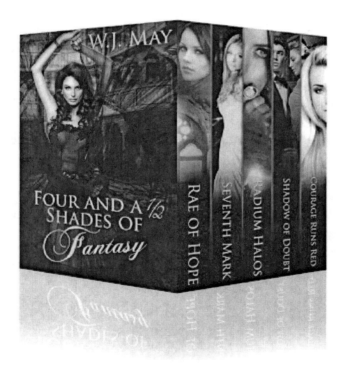

Four and a Half Shades of Fantasy

TUDOR COMPARISON:

Aumbry House—A recess to hold sacred vessels, often found in castle chapels.

Aumbry House was considered very special to hold the female students - their sacred vessels (especially Rae Kerrigan).

Joist House—A timber stretched from wall-to-wall to support floorboards.

Joist House was considered a building of support where the male students could support and help each other.

Oratory—A private chapel in a house.

Private education room in the school where the students were able to practice their gifting and improve their skills. Also used as a banquet - dance hall when needed.

Oriel—A projecting window in a wall; originally a form of porch, often of wood. The original bay windows of the Tudor period. Guilder College majority of windows were oriel.

Rae often felt her life was being watching through one of these windows. Hence the constant reference to them.

Refectory—A communal dining hall. Same termed used in Tudor times.

Scriptorium—A Medieval writing room in which scrolls were also housed.

Used for English classes and still store some of the older books from the Tudor reign (regarding tatùs).

Privy Council—Secret council and "arm of the government" similar to the CIA, etc... In Tudor times, the Privy Council was King Henry's board of advisors and helped run the country.

Don't miss out!

Click the button below and you can sign up to receive emails whenever W.J. May publishes a new book. There's no charge and no obligation.

Did you love *Mark of Fate*? Then you should read *Christmas Before the Magic* by W.J. May!

Learn how it all began ... before the magic of tatùs.

When Argyle invites his best friend, Simon Kerrigan, home for the Christmas holidays, he wants to save Simon from staying at Guilder Boarding School on his own.

Simon comes along and doesn't expect to find much more excitement in the tiny Scottish town where Argyle's family lives. Until he meets Beth, Argyle's older sister. She's beautiful, brash and clearly interested in him.

When her father warns him to stay away from her, Simon tries, but sometimes destiny has a hope of it's own.